THE
BLACK SHIP

with

Other Allegories and Parables

by

Elizabeth Rundle Charles

NATAL PUBLISHING LLC
ARS LONGA, VITA BREVIS

CONTENTS

The Black Ship

THEY lived at the foot of the Pine Mountains, in the island of the King's Garden, the mother, with her little son and daughter. The boy's name was Hope, and the little girl's, May.

The children loved each other dearly, and were never separated. They never had any quarrels, because Hope was the leader in all their expeditions and plays; and May firmly believed that everything which Hope planned and did, was better planned and better done than it would have been by any one else in the world, by which May meant the island. Hope, on his side, had always a tender consideration for little May in his schemes, such as kings should have for their subjects. May would never have dreamed of originating any scheme herself, or of questioning any which Hope planned. If you had taken away May from Hope, you would have taken away his kingdom, his army, his right hand; if you had taken away Hope from May, you would have robbed her of her leader, her king, her head, her sun. Bereaved of May, I think Hope would have been driven from his desolate home into the wide world; bereaved of Hope, I am sure May would never have left her home, but sat silent there until she pined away. But together, life was one holiday to them; work was a keener kind of play, and every day was too narrow for the happy occupations of which each hour was brimful.

Their cottage was at the foot of the mountains, on the sea-shore. Indeed, every house and cottage in the island stood on the sea-shore, because the island was so long and narrow, that, from the top of the mountain range which divided it, you could see the sea on both sides. If in any place the coast widened, little creeks ran in among the hills, and made the sea accessible from all points. The island consisted entirely of this one mountain range towering to the clouds; the higher peaks covered with snow, with a strip of coast at their feet, sometimes narrowing to a little shingly beach, sometimes expanding to a fertile plain, where beautiful cities with fairy bell-towers and marble palaces gleamed like ivory carvings amidst the palms and thick green trees.

But Hope and May knew nothing of the island beyond

the little bay they lived in, and no one they had ever seen or heard of had scaled the mountain range and looked on the other side; no one, either in the scattered fishermen's huts around them, or in the white town which perched like a sea-bird on the crags on the opposite side of the bay. Indeed, it was only from their mother's words that the children knew their country was an island; and ever since they had heard this, the great subject of Hope's dreams, and the great object of his schemes, had been to scale the mountains and look on the other side. But this was quite a secret between Hope and May; the happy secret which formed the endless interest of their long talks and rambles, but which they could not speak of to their mother, because she was so tenderly timid about them, and because it was to be the great surprise which one day was to enchant her, when Hope was a man. He was to scale the mountains, penetrate to the wondrous land on the other side, and bring thence untold treasures and tales of marvels to May and his mother.

The children thought Hope would very soon be old enough to go; and they had a little cave in the rocks close to the sea where they treasured up dried fruits and bits of iron to make tools of with which to chop away the tangled branches in the forests, and cut steps in the glaciers which Hope was to traverse. The lower hills the children knew well; and the ravine which wound up far among the hills they had nearly fixed on as the commencement of the journey.

So the days passed on with the children, rich in purposes and bright with happy work. For they were helpful to their mother. From their mountain expeditions they brought her firewood, and forest-honey, and eggs of wild-fowl, and various sweet wild-berries, and wholesome roots. They always noticed that their mother encouraged these mountain expeditions, and seemed much happier when they took that direction than when they kept by the sea.

Once Hope had said to her—

"Mother, how beautiful our country is! And I think it is so happy always to be in sight of the sea. How dull those lands must be you tell us of which are so large that many people have to live out of hearing of the waves! I could not bear to live there; it must seem so narrow and close to be shut in on the land with nothing beyond. But here we can never get out of sight of the sea. May and I always find, wherever we roam among the hills, we never lose the sea. When we wander far back from the shore, the beautiful blue waters seem to follow us as if they loved us; and in the inmost recesses of the mountains we always see beneath us some glimpse of bright water in the creeks, which run up among the hills, or the rivers which come down to meet them. The sea seems to love every corner of our country, mother, and penetrate everywhere."

A cold shudder passed over the mother's frame, and tears gathered in her eyes.

"The sea is indeed everywhere, my children," she murmured, and then with a burst of irresistible emotion she clasped them to her heart, and added bitterly, "Happy the country which that sea cannot approach!"

May and Hope wondered greatly at her words; but there was something in her manner which awed them into silence. For some time after that, they often speculated together as to what her words could mean, a vague terror seemed to murmur in the ripple of the waves. But gradually the impression wore off in the happy forgetfulness of childhood, and their old schemes were resumed with the same zest as before.

One evening, however, as they were busied with their treasures in the cave, the tide surprised them, and when they set out to return home, they found the rocky point which separated them from their cottage surrounded with deep water. The sides of the cliff in the little cove where their cave lay were sheer precipices of smooth rock, too steep to climb, so that the children had to wait some hours before they could creep round the point. Eagerly they watched the declining sun and the retreating tide, and when the waves were only ankle-deep they bounded through them, and in a few minutes were at the cottage door.

It was not yet dark, and the children were dancing into the cottage full of spirits at their adventure, when they were startled at the appearance of their mother. She was leaning, stony and motionless, with fixed eyes and clasped hands, against the doorpost, and for a moment the sight of her darlings did not seem to rouse her. Then springing up with a wild cry, she strained them to her heart, covered them with kisses, laughed a wild laugh, broken with convulsive sobs, and at last fell fainting on the floor.

The children knelt beside her, and gradually she revived, and fell into a sleep. But every now and then she started as if with some terrible dream, and murmured in her sleep, "The ship—the Black Ship; not now, not yet; take me, not them; or take us all—take us all!"

The terrified children could not sleep, and all the next day they clung close to their mother, and scarcely spoke a word. In the evening, however, she rallied, and tried to speak cheerfully and account for her alarm.

"You were late, darlings; and I knew you were by the sea—the terrible sea."

But the children could not be comforted. They felt the weight of some vague apprehension; they could not be tempted to leave their mother; they crept noiselessly about, watching her movements. Until at last one night they whispered together, and resolved to take courage and ask their mother what made her dread the sea; and then they consulted long as to the best way of introducing the forbidden subject.

The next evening, as they sat together by the fireside, Hope began, and forgetting all the speeches they had prepared, fixed his large eyes on his mother's, and said abruptly, "Mother, what is there terrible in the sea?"

She paused a moment, her face grew deadly pale, and her lips trembled.

"Children, why should you wish to know? You will learn too soon without my telling you."

"O mother, tell us," said May. "We can bear anything from you. Do not let any one else tell us."

A sudden thought seemed to flash across her, and she said, "Children, you are right."

Then folding one arm around Hope as he stood by her, and taking May on her knee, she said, "It is not the sea I dread; it is the Black Ship. That is the terrible secret; and it is, indeed, better you should learn it from my lips than learn it by losing me, and no one be left to tell you how.

"My children," she continued, making a great effort to

speak calmly, "this is the one sorrow of our country. From time to time a Black Ship, without sails or oars, glides silently to our shores, and anchors there. A dark, veiled Figure lands from it, and seizes any one of our people whom it chooses, without violence, without a sound, but with irresistible power, and quietly leads the victim away to the Ship, which immediately glides away again from our coasts as swiftly and noiselessly as it came; but no one ever sees those who are thus borne away any more."

"Whence does the Ship come, mother?" asked Hope, after a long silence. "And whither does it go?"

"No one knows, my child. That is the terrible thing about it. There is no sound nor voice. The agonised cries of those who are thus bereaved avail not to bring one word of reply from those lips, or to raise one fold of that dark veil. If we only knew, we could bear it."

"Have you ever seen it, mother?" asked Hope, determined bravely to plunge to the bottom of the terrible mystery, while May could only cling round her mother's neck and cry.

"I have seen it twice," she replied, speaking low and rapidly. "We did not always live here. Your father was rich and a man of rank, and loving us most dearly, he resolved to do all in his power to keep the terrible Form away. For this end, he built that castle you have often seen above the white tower. It is far above the sea; the rocks are perpendicular; it is built of solid stone; the doors were of oak, studded with iron; the windows barred with iron. No one was ever to be permitted to cross the moat without being strictly scrutinised. The gates were always to be closed.

"When it was finished, he made a feast. And after it, when the guests had left, and every bolt was drawn, we stood at the window of the room where you slept, and looked down triumphantly on the sea. A little sister of yours was sleeping in my arms. In the bay at our feet was moored the Black Ship. Our eyes seemed fascinated to it, and we could not speak. We saw the Veiled Figure; descend the side, and slowly scale the precipice beneath us, as if it had been a road made for it to tread. It walked over the waters of the castle moat, which did not seem to wet its feet. It stood on the balcony outside our window, and we could not stir. It passed through the iron bars. It laid its hand on my sleeping babe.

"Your father's strong arm was around us both, but before we could utter a cry, the darling had glided like a shadow from our embrace. The bright face of our baby was hidden from us under the folds of that impenetrable veil. We watched the terrible Form noiselessly descend the steep, re-enter the ship, and not until the Black Ship was already gliding swiftly out of sight could we overcome the terrible fascination. Then my cries of agony awoke the household, boats were manned in pursuit, but in vain, in vain—we felt it was in vain. We never saw the babe again."

She spoke with the languor of a sorrow which had been overwhelmed by greater sorrows still.

"But our father?" asked Hope.

"He left the castle the next day," she answered; "we never returned to it. He said the strong walls only mocked our helplessness, and since then the castle has been empty. Birds build their nests in our chambers, wild beasts make their lair in our gardens, the iron bars rust on the open doors; and if the Veiled Figure enters again, it will find no prey."

"But where did you go?"

"We came here. Your father said he would dare the foe, and, since no fortification could keep it out, meet it on its own ground. So he built this cottage close to the sea, and here we have lived ever since. I was content to remain here, because I thought we might avoid seeing anyone, and keep the terrible secret from you.

"And here," she continued with the calmness of despair, "one morning we saw the Black Ship moored, and your father went to meet it. I wept and clung to him to keep him back, but he said, 'It shall speak to me.'

"The Dark Form came up, a black shadow across the sunny beach. Your father encountered it boldly, and said, 'Where is my child?'

"There was no sound in reply. For a moment there seemed to be a struggle. I rushed towards them, but the terrible touch was on your father's hand. There seemed no violence, no chain was on his arm—only that paralysing touch. He went from me silent and helpless as the babe.

"'Whither, whither?' I cried. 'Only tell me where!'

"He looked back once, but he spoke to me no more. I rushed madly into the sea, but the ship was gone in a minute, and your voices, your baby voices, called me back, and I came."

"Is there no help, mother?" said Hope, at last. "Has no one ever tried? If I were but a man! Oh, surely some help could be found?"

"So thousands have thought, tried, and asked in vain. Fleets have scoured the seas, but none ever came on the Black Ship's track. Have you seen that line of surge far out on the sea?"

"The reef, mother? Yes; we have often wondered what it was."

"It is the great sea-wall which our people built ages since. The whole nation combined once to encircle the island with a gigantic sea-wall which no ship might pass. On the day of its completion, there was a great national festival on the sea-shore. But at noon-day, as they danced and feasted, one who was watching saw a black speck on the horizon.

"The festivities were suspended, and every one gathered on the beach to look. It grew larger and darker—it came to the sea-wall—without a moment's pause it glided through, and the multitude could gaze no longer. They scattered in all directions to their homes; and before morning, from hundreds of families, one was gone—princes, nobles, peasants—one sweeping yet terribly discriminating desolation. But in the sea-wall not the smallest breach could be found. Since then it has never been repaired, and the waves have worn it down to a broken reef, over which our boats pass freely."

Hope was silenced, and the little family sat up together that night. They did not dare to separate, even to their beds, yet before long, the children were asleep.

Sleep revived the brother and sister. And by the evening, Hope's ardent heart had found another point to rest on.

"Mother," he said, "if we could only find out whence the Black Ship comes, we might be comforted. Perhaps it comes from a happy place. Can no one even guess?"

"There are some who profess to know something of it," she replied; "but your father never believed them."

"Who are they?" asked Hope.

"The amulet-makers. There are a band of men in the White Town, and one of them in many of the villages, who profess to know something of the country from which the Black Ship comes, and who sends it. But they talk very mysteriously, in learned words; and I do not understand them. Your father said it was all a deception; because some of them profess to make amulets or charms which keep the Veiled Form away; and your little sister had one round her neck when she was taken from us. You have each one, but I cannot trust it; and I never could find out that the amulet-makers had anything but guesses as to where the ship came from; and your father said we could guess as well as they.

"There is one thing," she added, with a faint smile, "which gives me more comfort than anything they ever said. When our baby was taken from my arms—when she felt that terrible touch—she did not seem to be at all afraid. She looked up in my face, and then at the Veiled Form, and stretched out her baby arms from me to it, and smiled. At first, I hated to think of that. It seemed as if some cruel charm was on her to win even her heart from me; but often in the night, in my dreams, that smile has come back to me, like a promise; and I have awaked, comforted—I hardly know why."

"Perhaps they are in a happy place, mother," said little May.

And Hope said—"Mother, I am going to question the amulet-makers in the White Town."

And his mother suffered him to go.

In two days, Hope came back. But his step was spiritless and slow, and his face very sad.

"Mother," he said, "I think my father was right. I am afraid no one knows anything about the country from which the Black Ship comes. At first the amulet-makers promised to tell me a great deal. Some of them told me they believed it was a great king, an enemy of our race, who sent the ship; but that if we kept certain rules, and put on a certain dress they would sell us, or give them certain treasures to throw into the sea when the Ship appeared, they would watch for us, and make the powers beyond the sea favourable to us. But when I came to the question—how they knew this to be true, or if they had ever had any message from beyond the sea, or seen any one who came thence, they grew silent, and sometimes angry, and told me I was a presumptuous child.

"There was one old man, however, who was kind to me; and he came and spoke to me alone, and said, 'My child, be happy to-day—to be good is to be happy. What is beyond to-day, or beyond the sea, no one knows, or ever can know. Go back to your mother, and live as before.' So I came," concluded Hope. "But it can never, never be with us again as before we knew."

From that time the boy seemed to cease to be a child, or to take interest in any childish schemes. He was gentle and tender as his father could have been to his mother and to May, and seemed to take on himself to watch over and protect them. He never left them out of sight.

Until, one day, as they came, in their ramble in search of shell-fish, on their old cave, and looked once more at their little stores, so joyously hoarded there, May suddenly exclaimed, "What if they should know on the other side of the mountains!"

The thought flashed on Hope like a breath of new life; and from that day his old schemes were resumed, but with an intensity and a purpose which could not be quenched. He would scale the mountains, to see if any tidings from beyond the sea had reached the land across the mountains!

His mother's consent was gained; and in a few days, spent in eager preparations, Hope was to start.

But before those days were ended, one evening, a white-haired old man knocked at the cottage door. He was nearly exhausted with travel, his clothes were torn, and his feet bleeding.

They led him to the fire, bathed his feet, and set food before him. But before he would touch anything, the old man said—

"I have tidings for you—glad tidings."

"Do you come from across the mountains?" exclaimed Hope, starting to his feet.

The old man bowed in assent.

"I come from across the mountains, and I bring you glad tidings from beyond the sea."

"Glad tidings!" they all exclaimed.

"Glad tidings, if you will obey them," he replied;—"if not, the saddest you ever heard. It is not an enemy who sends the Black Ship, but a friend."

Not a question, scarcely a breath interrupted him; and he continued, in brief, broken sentences—

"It is our King. Our island belongs to Him. He gave it us. But, long ago, our people rebelled against Him. They were seduced by a wicked prince, His deadly enemy, and, alas! ours. They sent the King a defiance; they defaced His statues, which were a type of all beauty; they broke His laws, which are the unfolding of all goodness. He sent ambassadors to reclaim them; He, who could have crushed the revolt, and destroyed our nation with one of His armies in a day, descended from His dignity, and stooped to entreat our deluded people to return to their allegiance. But they treated his condescension as weakness. They defied His ambassadors, and maltreated them and drove them from the island. He had warned them against the usurper, and told them the consequences of revolting; and too surely they have been fulfilled.

"The Black Ship is the punishment inflicted by our offended Monarch; but those who return to His allegiance need not dread it."

"Some, then, have submitted to the King?" asked Hope.

"Every ambassador He sent has persuaded some to recognise the King."

"Why not all?" asked Hope. "If the King is good and is our King, and will receive us, why not all return?"

"The usurper seduces them still," replied the old man. "Many hate the King's good laws; many take pride in what they call their independence; most will not listen, or will not believe. They mock the King's messengers, and declare that they are impostors, that their messages are a delusion, and some even persist in declaring that there is no King, and no country beyond the sea."

"But the Black Ship is not a delusion!" said Hope. "It must come from some land. What proof have these ambassadors given? Have they ever been in the land beyond the sea?"

"They gave many proofs, but I bring you better news than this. A few years since, the King's Son came Himself. Many of us have seen and spoken with Him. He stayed many days. He spoke words of such power, and in tones of such tenderness as none who heard can ever forget. We could trace in His features the lineaments of the statues we had defaced. Some of the worst rebels among us were melted to repentance, and fell at His feet, and besought His pardon. I was one.

"He gave us not only His pardon, but His friendship. But His enemies prevailed. Especially the amulet-makers organised a conspiracy against Him; they feared for their trade, and secretly prepared to drive Him from the island. He had come alone, for He came not to compel but to win. And He came for another purpose, which, until He was gone, we could not comprehend. The conspirators triumphed. One day they came in force and seized Him. Alas, a base panic seized us who loved Him, and we fled.

"They bound Him with thongs, they treated Him with the most barbarous cruelty and the basest indignity and drove Him to the sea. We thought a fleet and an army would have appeared to avenge His insulted majesty, and proclaim him King with power, or bear Him in pomp away. But to our surprise and dismay, nothing came for Him but the Black Ship, and the Dark Form bore Him from us, as if He had been a rebel like one of us.

"He had told us something of the probability of this before it happened, but we could not comprehend what He meant. Never were days of such sorrow as those which passed over us after His being taken from us. His enemies were in full triumph; they mocked our Prince's claims, they insulted us, they threatened us, but all they could say or do was nothing in comparison with the anguish in our hearts.

"For what could we think? He we had loved and trusted was gone, borne off in triumph by the very foe He came to deliver us from. We hid ourselves in caves and lonely beaches by the sea, and recalled to each other His precious words, and gazed out over the sea with a vague yearning, which was scarcely hope, and yet kept us lingering on the shore.

"On the third morning, in the gray light of early dawn,

one of us saw Him on the shore—one who had owed Him everything, and loved Him most devotedly. She called us to come. One by one we gathered round Him. Some of us could scarcely believe our senses for joy. But it was Himself; the solid certainty of that unutterable joy grew stronger. And then He told us wonders, how He suffered all this for us—had borne this indignity and captivity in obedience to His Father's will, to set us free—had gone in the Black Ship itself to the heart of the enemy's country, and alone trodden those terrible regions of lawless wickedness to which he seeks to drag his deluded victims, and alone vanquished him there.

"He stayed with us some days, and talked with us familiarly, as of old; but how glorious His commonest words were—how overpowering His forgiving looks—how inspiring His firm and tender tones, I can never tell. He could not remain with us then. He said we must be His messengers, and win back His rebels to allegiance; we must learn to be brave, to speak and suffer for Him, and to act as men; and He promised to come again one day with fleets and armies, and all the pomp of His Father's kingdom.

"But, meantime, He said the Black Ship should never more be a terror to any of us who loved Him; for He himself would come in it each time. He would be veiled, so that none could see Him but the one He came for; but surely as the Black Ship came, instead of the Dark Form, He would come Himself for every one of us, and bear us home to His Father's house to abide with Him, and with Him hereafter to return."

There was a breathless silence, broken only by the mother's sobs.

She clasped her hands, and murmured—

"Then it was He—it was surely He himself who came and took my babe. No wonder my darling smiled, and was willing to go."

The mother and the children that very evening received from the stranger the medal which was worn by all those who returned to their allegiance. It was a Black Ship, surrounded with rays of glory, and behind it the towers of a city.

Never were a happier company than the four who gathered round the cottage table that evening. They were too happy, and had too much to ask, to sleep. And far into the night the questions and answers continued, every reply of the old man's only revealing some fresh endearing excellence in the King and the King's Son, until they longed for the Black Ship to come and fetch them home.

"If only," said little May, "it would fetch us all at once!"

"That the King will do when He comes with His armies in the day of His triumph. Till then, my child, this is the one only sorrow connected with the Black Ship for those who love the King. We go one by one, and blessed as it is for the one who goes, it must be sad sometimes for those who are left."

"Why do not those who go to Him ask Him to come quickly?" asked Hope.

"They do," replied the old man. "'Come quickly' is the entreaty of all who love Him here and beyond the sea; but His time is best. And, meantime, have we forgotten the multitudes who are still deceived by the usurper, to whom the Black Ship is still a horrible end of all things, and the Veiled Form of the King of Terrors?"

Hope rose and stood before the old man.

"Mother," he said, "it is for this we must live. Think of the desolate hearts in the homes around us. Think of the thousands who know not our blessed secret in the White Town."

The old man rose and laid his hand on Hope's head.

"My King!" he said. "When wilt Thou come for me? Is not my work done? Will not this youthful voice speak for Thee here as my quivering tones no longer can? Wilt Thou not come? I have many dear ones with Thee; but when Thou wilt is best."

Then he persuaded them all to lie down to rest, and he himself composed himself quietly to sleep.

But in the night, a wondrous light filled the room—a wondrous light and fragrance. The mother woke, and the children, and they saw the old man standing, gazing towards the door, which was open. There stood a Veiled Form, dark to the mother's eyes as the dreaded form she knew too well; yet its presence filled the room with the light as of a rosy dawn, and the fragrance as of spring flowers. The old man's hair was silvery, and his form tottering as ever, but in his face there was the beauty of youth, and in his eyes the rapture of joy.

"Farewell, my friends," he said; "your day of joy will come like this of mine. Thou art come for me at last—Thou thyself. I see Thy face, I hear Thy voice; I come—it is Thou."

A hand was laid tenderly on his hand, and they walked away together into the night.

But as the mother and children looked after him from the door, they saw the Black Ship, only at its prow was a star. And as it passed away, the mother, and Hope, and May thought it left a track of light upon the sea.

The three had henceforth enough to live and suffer for. To the lonely fishermen's huts went May and her mother, into the White Town went Hope, and everywhere they bore their tidings of joy. They had much to suffer, and many mocked, and against them also the amulet-makers combined, and would not listen. But some did listen, and believe, and love, and to such, as to the mother, and Hope, and May, the Black Ship, instead of a phantom of terror, became a messenger of surpassing joy.

THE RUINED TEMPLE

THE Temple was in ruins, and the Priestess sat, a captive in chains, among its broken and scattered fragments.

It had been a temple of the most ancient form, open to the sky, beautiful beyond any temple upon earth, beautiful and sacred, and some remnants of its beauty hung about it still—fragments of exquisite carvings and broken shafts of graceful columns. But everything was shattered and out of place, the window tracery shivered in a thousand fragments and strewn on the ground, columns prostrate, sacred vessels lying rusted among the weeds, the pure spring which had gushed from beneath the altar choked up and dry, and instruments of sacred music mute and broken on the ground.

On the walls in some places were the traces of violence, but it was remarkable that they seemed to have been assaulted only from within. Indeed, the temple had been a fortress, so impregnably situated and built, that except from within, not one stone could ever have been displaced.

This was, in fact, the saddest part of its history. The temple had been desecrated before it had been ruined, and in its ruin it was a temple still, but, alas! no longer sacred to Him in whose honour it had been reared.

Many senseless or loathsome idol-images were carved on the walls, strangely contrasting, in their shapelessness or deformity, with the symmetry of every fragment of the original structure. On the broken altar in the centre stood an image of the Priestess herself. This was the earliest idol which had entered there, and with the entrance of this, the ruin had begun. The Enemy who had, with subtle flatteries, introduced this idol, had ever since had access to the temple, and step by step the Priestess had sunk beneath his power. He had led her into wild orgies, in which she herself had defaced the delicate tracery and torn down the walls; and when she awoke from the frenzy and wept, as sometimes she would, he silenced her tears with blows or with mocking threats of the vengeance of Him to whom the temple had been consecrated.

Sometimes, however, she woke to a moment's full

consciousness of the desolation around her, and then she would wail and lament until he seemed to fear some unseen Friend would hear; and at such seasons he grew more gentle, and renewed the old persuasions and flatteries by which he had misled her first. He would even encourage her at times, when all other methods failed, to try and collect the scattered stones, and repair the breaches in the shattered walls and re-string the broken harp, for he knew well her puny efforts must fail, and that no hands but those of the builder could ever restore the ruin she had wrought.

So, after a few faint endeavours, she, as he expected, would give up in despair, and sit cowering hopelessly on the ground afraid of him, afraid of Him whose priestess she was, afraid of her own voice.

In such bitter hours, he would again grow bold, and mock her with the memory of the past, until the spirit of indignant resistance seemed roused within her, when, once more softening his tone, he would point her with flattering words to her own image on the broken altar. He would shew her the beauty still lingering in its marred and weather-worn features, and help her to decorate it with gay colours and tinsel ornaments, placing in her hands the golden censer, with the sweet incense which had been made in happier days for far other uses; and she would wave the fragrant compound before the idol image of herself.

But with the pure spices which made it sweet, the enemy had mixed a narcotic poison, and as she languidly swung the censer to and fro, her brain would become intoxicated with the voluptuous sweetness, until, in a dream of vain delight, she would fall asleep, and forget all her miseries. And ever, as she slept, he would rivet faster the chain which, unperceived by her, was being bound around her, every year making her range of action narrower and her movements less free.

Wild beasts, also, made their lair in the desolate temple-chambers, prowling in and out where formerly meek and heavenly beings had ministered, and making the shattered walls echo with their loud howls and sullen roarings, where once had sounded strains of pure and joyous music.

Thus, day by day, the ruin spread, and the desolation and

desecration became more complete.

But it happened one spring, that two little singing-birds came back from the sunny clime where they had wintered, and began building their nest above the ancient altar. There was something in the spring-time which often brought tears to the eyes of the fallen priestess, she scarcely knew why. The world seemed then like one happy temple full of thankful songs; and as, day by day, the sun repaired the ruins of winter, and the choral services of the woods took a fuller tone, on her heart there fell the mournful sense of the ruins around her, which no spring-tide could restore. Yet something of a softer feeling, a melancholy which breathed of hope, stole over her, and she watched those two happy birds building their nest, and warbling as they worked.

At last, the nest was finished, the happy mother-bird sat on her eggs, and the pair had much leisure for confidential conversation.

"How desolate this place is," said the mother-bird.

"And it was once so beautiful," replied her mate.

"Why is it not rebuilt?" she asked.

"None can rebuild but the hand that built," was the mysterious reply.

"But would not the architect come if asked? He is so good. Was it not he who taught us to build our nest; and I am sure nothing can be better done than that."

"That is the difficulty," was the reply. "The priestess does not know he is so good, and is afraid to utter his name. If she only called him, he would come."

"Is he near enough?"

"He is always near."

"Are you sure?" said the mother-bird. "What can we do to help her?"

"I do not know," replied the mate, "except it is to sing his praise. Perhaps she may listen, and understand one day how good he is."

So all the spring, the little happy creatures chirped and sang, until the nestlings were fledged, and the whole family flew away.

But their songs had penetrated deep into the priestess' heart. And one night, when the Enemy was absent, and the wild beasts prowling far away, she threw herself on the earth before her desecrated altar, and lamented and wept. But for the first time her lamentations, instead of solitary, hopeless wailings, echoing back from the ruined walls, became a broken cry for help.

"Thou, if thou art indeed so good—if thou art indeed near, come and help me," she sobbed; "repair my ruins, and save me."

And for the first time, as she wept and implored, she felt the weight of her fetters binding hand and foot, and, clasping her chained hands, she cried more earnestly, "Come and set me free!"

And before the day dawned, a voice came softly through the silence—

"I will come."

But with the morning light, how bitter was the sight which burst on her aching eyes! All had been as desolate long before; but she had never seen it as she saw it now. Noisome beasts, which prowled fearlessly around her; skulls and ghastly skeletons of their murdered prey strewn about; on the ground the broken, rusted harp; on her hands the heavy chain; and, worse than all, the door she had opened to the Enemy ever open, and inviting his approach.

Too surely he came. He mocked her hope until it appeared baseless as a dream; and nothing seemed real, but the ruin to which he scornfully directed her gaze, and the chain which now, for the first time without concealment, he held up triumphantly, dragging her by it to every corner of the polluted and ruined temple, to show her how complete and hopeless the ruin was. Then drawing the links tighter than before, so that they galled and wounded her wrists, he led her to the image of herself, which he had adorned, and painted, and so often flattered. He dragged off the tinsel ornaments, and effaced the delusive colouring, and left her, at last, face to face with the defaced and broken idol, saying—

"This is the worship you yourself have chosen. Pursue it still. There is no other for you."

She could not bear to gaze on it; and as he went, she fell

prostrate on the altar steps, and hid her face on the stones. Yet still, though with but a feeble hope, she sobbed out—

"If thou art good—if thou canst help me, come,—oh, come, and set me free!"

Weariness at last brought sleep, and in her dreams she saw a lovely vision of the temple as it once had been. White columns gleamed, sweet and solemn music sounded, and she herself ministered in white robes at the altar, before a Radiant Form, on which she could scarcely for a moment gaze.

The awaking from this dream to the desolation around her was more terrible than all she had felt before. It must have bereft her of reason, but for the echo of three cheering words, which seemed to have awakened her—

"I will come."

The next day, with the light of that radiant vision on her heart, she dragged her fettered limbs to the altar, and strove with her feeble and trembling hands to tear that marred image from the shrine. But in vain. It was too firmly imbedded there; and she could only turn her face from it, and weep, and cry for help.

And before the next morning's dawn, help came.

In the night, a heavenly visitant descended; and with human words, in a language she had not spoken for years, but every word of which melted her heart like the accents of her mother-tongue, he touched her chains, and they fell off.

He spoke, and the wild beasts fled, howling; he touched her broken harp, and it was restrung and tuned; he touched the dry and choked up channel of the sacred spring, and it welled forth pure and fresh from beneath the altar; he touched the idol on the shrine, and it fell, and in its stead shone that wondrous Radiance which she had seen in her dream. Then he poured on her head the fragrant oil of consecration, and clothed her in a white vestal priestly garment, and placed the restrung harp in her hand, and rose again to heaven.

At first her joy knew no measure. She gazed on the sacred shrine, and in its glory at times she perceived the lineaments of the form of Him who had done all this for her. She touched her harp, and the sweet strings responded as if they knew her hand; she sang holy songs in that old, long-forgotten, yet familiar tongue, so heavenly and happy that the wild beasts would not venture near, and the morning-birds were silent to listen. She bathed in the newly-opened fountain and drank of it, and as she drank, her strength and her youth came back.

For a time her joy was without cloud or measure; but as the daylight returned, the desolation or the ruined temple struck sadly on her heart. It was indeed a sacred place once more, and she its consecrated priestess; but was this ruin never to be repaired?

She began to cleanse the sacred vessels and to sweep the earth of all the refuse and dry bones which had been gathered there. And then, with her renewed strength, she set herself to collect the broken fragments of the columns, and tried to piece together the shattered tracery and the delicate carvings of flower and foliage. But it was in vain. She could indeed bring the shattered fragments together and see what they had been, but she could not join them, or replace one prostrate shaft or capital.

And as she sat down mournfully before her shrine, tears dimmed her eyes, so that she could scarcely see the Radiance there, and, falling on her harp-strings, would have rusted them and marred their sweetness; whilst in the silence, a voice, too long and bitterly familiar, was heard at the door. Turning round, she perceived the form of the Enemy there, whilst behind him glared fierce and hungry eyes, and in her terror, the harp almost fell from her hands.

But she threw herself on her knees before the altar, pressed the harp convulsively to her heart, and cried, "Will these ruins never be repaired, these doors never closed against my enemy and thine?"

The pressure of her trembling fingers drew forth some plaintive strains, like the wind on Æolian strings; but low and plaintive as they were, the enemy disappeared, and the wild beasts fled howling from them.

Then she began to perceive the power of her harp, and drew from it a song of joy and triumph. And as she still gazed on the radiant shrine, a veil seemed to be withdrawn from it, and she perceived that it was a window, so that the light streamed through it, not from it.

Wondering, she gazed, until, penetrating further and further through the light, she saw in the depths of heaven a Temple like her own, only perfect, glorious beyond comparison, and full;—full of worshippers robed and singing like herself, and full of that wondrous radiance which streamed from the heavenly form she had seen.

She laid her harp upon the shrine, and to her surprise the strings began to quiver of their own accord. An electric current united them to the harps in the heavenly temple, and they vibrated in exquisite harmonies the echo of the harmonies above.

And with the heavenly strains, came a voice divine and human, mighty as the sound of many waters, yet soft and near as a whisper in her ear:

"Here all ruins are repaired, the enemy cannot enter here, but here thou shalt dwell for ever."

And softly floated down these other words:—

"For we know that if our earthly house of this tabernacle were dissolved, we have a building of God, an house not made with hands, eternal in the heavens."

THE JEWEL OF THE ORDER OF THE KING'S OWN

ONCE on the sea-shore, in a land a long way off, I met an old man dressed as a galley-slave, and toiling at convicts' work, with a heavy chain around one of his arms; but his face and bearing were stamped with the truest nobility. I felt sure he must be a victim of some political cabal, and not a criminal, for not a trace of crime or remorse debased that calm brow and those clear, honest eyes. This might not have struck me as remarkable, since such unmerited sufferings were but too common in that country. What arrested my attention was the expression of unfeigned and lofty joy which irradiated his aged countenance.

In the interval of noon-day rest allowed him, as well as the other convicts, I sate down beside him and entered into conversation with him. I found he was an old soldier. And at length, I was encouraged by his frankness to inquire the cause of the strange contrast between his expression and his circumstances.

The veteran lifted his cap, and said mysteriously, "The King shall enjoy his own again. The spring will come, and with it the violets."

The thought struck me that some harmless and happy insanity had risen, like a soft mist, to veil from him his miserable lot. And, following his train of thought, I said, "You wait for a king, and hope cheers you. Yet you must have waited long; and hope deferred maketh the heart sick."

"The uncertainty of hope," he replied, "often makes the heart sick with fear of disappointment, but my hope is sure, and every day of delay certainly brings me nearer to it. Every night, as I look out from my convict's cell over the sea, before I lie down to sleep, I think before to-morrow the white sails of his fleet may stud the blue waters—for he will not return alone; and when morning dawns gray across the bare horizon, I am not cast down, because I know the morning we wait for will surely come at last."

"But," I said, reverently, and half hesitating to disturb his happy dream, "when that morning dawns will you still be here?"

"Here or there," he answered, solemnly. "Either with the few who look for him here, or with the countless multitudes who will accompany him thence."

Knowing how such legends of the return of exiled princes linger in the hearts of a nation, and wondering whether the old man spoke from the delusion of his own peculiar madness or of a tradition current among his people, I said, "Your words are strange to me. Tell me the history."

"After the great battle," the old soldier replied, a smile bright as a child's, yet tender as tears, lighting up his whole countenance—"after the last great battle, the King, the true King, our own King, has never been seen publicly in our country. They wounded him, and left him for dead on the field—they had wounded his heart to the core. Traitors were amongst them; it was not only an open enemy that did him this dishonour. But they were mistaken; he is not dead. We who loved him know. We bore him secretly from the field. He lingered a few days amongst us after his wounds had healed, in disguise; but although his royal state was hidden for a time, we who knew his voice, could tell him blindfold from a million. And since he left us, his faithful adherents, who before his departure could be counted by tens, have increased to thousands."

"An unusual fortune," I remarked, "for a cause whose last effort seems generally to have been considered a defeat, and whose leader has apparently abandoned it."

"There are many reasons," said the old man, "why it should be so, and among the chief of these is this one. When our Prince left us, he gave to each of his adherents a precious gift as a token of his love, and a sign by which we may know each other."

As he spoke, he drew aside his poor garment, and on his breast there sparkled a gem more brilliant than any star or decoration I had ever seen.

"This is the star of the King's own order," he said.

And as I looked at it, a wonderful transformation seemed to have taken place in the old man's dress. His poor convict's garb seemed metamorphosed into the richest robes, such as princes wore in that southern land, of the costliest materials, and all of a glistening white, at once royal and bridal, whilst his chain glittered like a jewelled bracelet.

The veteran smiled at my surprise, and unclasping his jewel, bound it on his brow. Instantly the same magical change passed over his face. Noble as it was before, his countenance now shone as if it had been the face of an angel. Every trace of care or age was effaced, the eyes shone under the calm, unfurrowed brow with the sparkle of early youth, and nothing was left to indicate age but a depth in the glance and a history in the expression, which youth cannot have.

"But," I said, "surely your enemies must seek to rob you of such a treasure?"

"Try," he replied, "if you can take it from me."

I endeavoured gently to detach the jewel from his brow, but my fingers had scarcely touched it, when it sprang up like glittering drops from a fountain, and was gone, yet leaving the glory on the old man's face.

He smiled, and observed quietly, "Our jewel no man taketh from us."

Then, again unclasping the fillet which had bound it round his brow, the magic gem reappeared in his hand.

It was mid-day, and the usual fare of the convicts was brought to him —scanty and coarse fare, with bad water. He humbly and thankfully partook of the poor food, but poured out the contents of the cup on the ground.

"The water of this land is bad," he said. "The people render it palatable by mixing it with a fiery stimulant, which, alas! only increases their thirst, so that they ever thirst again; but we do not need this."

Then gently laying his finger on the gem, it expanded, like a lily-bell in the sun, into a crystal vase, and in it bubbled up a miniature fountain of pure, sparkling water.

"In us a well of water springing up," he murmured, as if to himself, as he drank and was refreshed. And touching the vase again, it folded up, like a convolvulus going to sleep when the sun sets.

I wondered he had not had the courtesy to offer me a draught.

He read my thoughts, and said, "This water is untransferable. Each of us must have his own jewel."

"Then," I replied, "if your Prince left those jewels to you at his departure, and has not returned since, how can his followers have increased, if this token is essential to them, and, indeed, as you intimated, an inducement to many to enlist under his banner?"

"It is free to all, and yet a secret," he replied. "Whenever any one desires to enlist in our Prince's service, he must repair alone, before daybreak, to a lonely beach on our shores, and wait there for what the King will send. There, when the sun rises, not always the first morning, or the second, or the third, but always at last, his first rays gleam on a new jewel, exactly like the others, sparkling among the shells and pebbles. The young soldier takes it up, presses it to his lips, murmurs the name written on it, binds it on his heart, and it is his own, and he is the King's for ever. None ever saw it come, though some fancy they have seen a streak of light on the sea when it first appears, as of the track of an illumination out on the waters."

"'What name is engraved on it?" I asked.

"The King's name," he replied, bowing his head reverently.

"May I see it," I said.

"You could not," he replied, gravely. "None of us can read that name, except on our own jewels."

I was silent for a moment.

He continued—

"But I have a greater wonder yet to tell you of our jewel—the greatest wonder of all; and this you must take at my word. The light and glory of this gem is entirely reflected from a jewel of the same kind, but infinitely more glorious, which sparkles on the King's own heart. When I raise this gem to my eyes, and look through it," he added in a tone which thrilled with the deepest emotion, raising it at the same time like a telescope to his eyes, "this country vanishes from me altogether, and I see wonders."

"What do you see?" I asked, half trembling.

"I see the King in his beauty," he replied. "I see the land which is very far-off. I see a city which has no need of the sun. I see a palace where his servants serve him. I see a throne which is as jasper, and, above it, a rainbow like an emerald;

and, above all I see, I see him, with the jewel on his heart; but his jewel is no mere gem, no reflection—it is a star, it is light itself; and in its richness the city, the palace, and the throne, and the happy faces of his servants round him, glow and shine."

And as he spoke, I looked at the old man's jewel, and his countenance itself grew so glorious, that I could not gaze any longer, but cast down my dazzled eyes, and was silent. At length, after a pause of some moments, my eagerness to hear more constrained me to resume the conversation. And when I looked up, the jewel was again hidden in the old man's breast, his appearance had taken its soberer beauty, and the presence of that marvellous treasure was only betrayed by the strange calm and peace which had first attracted me in the veteran's face.

"But," I asked, "if such a possession indeed is yours, the wonder now seems to me to be, how the King's enemies can have a follower left. Have your opponents any similar reward to offer?"

"Similar things," he replied, "they at one time often tried to make, but the same they could never have; and even to imitate the outside beauty of it, they found so difficult, that the soberest men of the party have, for the most part, given it up in despair, and say it is all a cheat."

"But why, at least, does not each one try for himself," I asked, "and see if it is true or not?"

"There are many reasons," he replied, sorrowfully, "which keep the land from returning nationally to its allegiance. The usurper is still in power, and gives away the offices of state as he pleases; bonds and imprisonments often await us, as you see is the case with me; and many prefer the possession of lands and houses, or even less, to the reversion of a city, and the service of a prince they have never seen."

"I understand," I replied.

"Besides," he added, "there are strict rules binding our order. The people of the usurper do each what is right in his own eyes; but we are subject to our Prince's laws, which, though most blessed to those who keep them, seem to those who are outside, and live lawlessly, severe and strict. We are subject to our Prince, and to one another for his sake; and only those who have proved the joy of that subjection and service know how much happier it is than the tyranny of their lawlessness and self-will."

"What are those counterfeit jewels you alluded to?" I asked.

"They are of various construction," he replied; "some try to imitate one quality of our jewel, and some another. Some of the court jewellers of the usurper make a paste or tinsel jewel, which, when the sun shines, has a lustre a little like that of ours. The young courtiers often wear this; but when the sun is clouded or sets, it ceases to shine, so that even its outward resemblance is very imperfect, and it does not even pretend to imitate the secret of the fountain or the magic glass. And, moreover, it can be stolen or broken: often, even in the courtly revels, it is broken; often it is stolen or dropped, and, even if it is retained, in a few years the lustre fades away and can never be restored.

"Then," he continued, "some made a bold effort to imitate our jewel in its form of the crystal vase, but the crystal itself is dim. And for the living fountain, they have never been able to substitute anything but a fiery liquid, needing constantly to be replenished, and, in reality, only increasing the thirst it professes to still, until it becomes a burning, consuming inward fever. But as they have never tasted of our water, the wretched deluded ones persist in saying theirs is the true."

"And the telescope?" I inquired—"The magic glass?"

"The telescope," he replied, with a smile, which had no mockery, but much sadness in it—"the magic glass they have never even attempted to imitate; and, therefore, as none can ever look through it but its possessor, they say it is a lie and a cheat. And our persisting in declaring what it really is, is the source of many of our sufferings. For this, we are thrown into madhouses and prisons, and led to the scaffold and the stake."

After a brief pause, he resumed—

"The wise men and statesmen of the usurper's party now, however, for the most part, take an entirely different method. They discourage all these counterfeits, which they say are paying a most undeserved compliment to us. They say our jewels are mere sham and tinsel; that the light they shed exists only in the fancy of the spectators; that the living water is nothing but a mirage; and that the visions we see through the telescope are simply a lie. They affect to despise us too much to punish us; and if they persecute us at all, it is simply by contemptuously shutting us up in asylums as enthusiasts—harmless, unless we mislead others.

"It is only a few of the most inveterate, such as myself; who may succeed in bringing over too many to the side of our King, that they occasionally make examples of, to sober the rest. But it is all entirely useless," he added, very joyfully; "the King's followers increase, his cause is gaining ground, and," he added, with a subdued voice, "the King himself is coming."

"Is it really true," I asked, after a time, "that nothing, or no man, can rob you of this treasure?"

"Our treasure no man taketh from us," he replied. "This he gave us, this he left with us: not as the world giveth, gave he unto us."

"But can nothing you yourselves do, or omit to do, spoil or dim your jewel?" I resumed.

His brow saddened.

"Alas! There and there only have our enemies any real strength against us," he replied. "Sorrows only add to its lustre; in the loss of everything else it only shines the brighter; hunger and thirst but prove the unfailing nature of the fountain in the crystal vase; destitution and darkness, dungeons and tortures, only make the bright visions of our telescope more glorious; but we, we ourselves may indeed dim its lustre, or, if we will, yield it up altogether."

"All this is natural and comprehensible," I said. "The dungeon must make the jewel brighter; the drought, the unfailing spring more precious; the narrowing of all prospects here, enhance the visions of that magic glass; the cruelties of the usurper, endear the sight of the Prince you serve."

"This the wisest of our enemies have found out," the old man replied. "They find that nothing they can do harms us, but only what they can make us do ourselves; and to this they direct their efforts."

"In what way?" I inquired.

"In many ways," he answered, sadly. "The jewel, which nothing external can dim, is sensitive to the least change in us. Any infringement of our King's laws, or, especially, any unfaithfulness to our King, dims its lustre at once; any drinking of these forbidden cups of intoxication dries up the crystal fountain; any yielding to the usurper's service blots out from our magic glass its glorious visions, and the sight of our King in his beauty."

"Are there any other dangers?" I inquired.

"Countless dangers," he replied. "Especially three devices have been found too successful against us. Our jewel only keeps bright with use, and in three ways our enemies endeavour to deter us from using it. The timid they threaten, and induce to hide it from fear: and the cowardly concealing of our treasure inflicts on us two evils: it prevents our winning by it fresh followers to our Prince; and in concealment the jewel itself invariably grows dim. The young and careless they engage in the ambitious pursuits or the gay amusements of the court, until they forget to use the precious gem, and in ceasing to use it, they necessarily cease to shine with its light, and grow like any of the usurper's train.

"And again, there are some poor, and distrusting, and fearful ones, whom our enemies persuade that it is a daring presumption for such as they to pretend they have had especial communication with the King, and even at times torment them into thinking the King's own jewel tinsel. So that, in looking and looking to see if it is a true jewel, they forget to clasp it on their hearts, or drink the living water, or look through the magic glass."

"That is a strange delusion," I remarked.

"Yes," he said; "but it is easily cured, if once we can persuade them to look through the jewel instead of looking at it; for then they see the King with the jewel on his breast, and the smile in his eyes, and their doubts melt away in floods of happy tears.

"This I know," he added, "for I was once one of these. I had neglected to use my jewel; and then an enemy, in the guise of a friend, persuaded me to question its genuineness; but I ventured to look through it once again, and since then, I do not look at my jewel, but gaze through it to the King's heart; and from that day, my jewel has not grown dim."

"But you spoke of some who lost it altogether," I said.

"They are those," he said, solemnly, "who have deliberately yielded it up to enter the service of the usurper, or those who, in base timidity, have cast it away in denying our King."

"And for such can it ever be recovered?" I said.

"For one such, as disloyal as any, it was," he answered. "He went out and wept bitterly; the King forgave him, and in time the treasure was restored to him, and he became one of our most glorious veterans."

"How is the jewel to be recovered if lost?" I asked.

"By going to the place where first it was found," he replied. "There, on the lonely beach, before daybreak, it must be sought, morning after morning, until the sun's first rays reveal it once more glittering among the shingle as at first. But the waiting is often longer than it was at first."

"Will you wear your jewel," I asked, "when the King comes, or when you go to join him beyond the sea?"

"There," he replied, with an expression of rapturous joy, "we shall see the jewel on the King's heart. There we shall have no need of the hidden fountain, for the river of living waters flows there, bright as crystal; and no need of the magic glass, for the King is near; but the jewel will shine in that happy place on brow and breast for ever and ever."

And as I left the sea-shore and the old man, these words floated through my heart, as if they were echoes of his history, or his story an echo of them:

"'Be not, as the hypocrites, of a sad countenance.'"

"'Peace I leave with you, my peace I give unto you: not as the world giveth, give I unto you.'"

"'Rejoice in the Lord always: and again I say, Rejoice.'"

"'Your joy no man taketh from you.'"

THE CATHEDRAL CHIMES: A LEGEND

IN a city whose history dates from the ages of silvery bells and stately buildings, there stood, and stands now for aught I know, a cathedral, rich in all the endless fancies of Gothic art. Inside, it was solemn with shade, and gorgeous with light which came in through the elaborate tracery of the stained windows, many-coloured, and broken as the sunbeams through a tropical forest. Outside, fretted pinnacles and carved bell-towers sprang upward, grand yet fairy-like, as if stone towers rose as easily and naturally towards heaven as oaks and pines. But the chief glory of this cathedral was its bells. They were the pride of the city, and the great attraction to strangers. Their history formed an important part of the civic chronicles.

A lady of a royal house had given them as a thank offering for her lord's safe return from the Crusades. All her silver-plate and ornaments, with spoils of Saracens from the recovered Holy Land, had been poured into the mould when they were made, so that from their birth all tender and sacred memories had been fused into their very essence, and their first tones echoed far-off times and lands.

A bishop who afterwards suffered martyrdom in the hands of African Moslems had blessed them. Their first peal had sounded in honour of a great victory. They had summoned the people through ages of conflict to defend their liberties. They had blended their life with the life of every home,—in family joys and family sorrows, at wedding, christening, and funeral. They had made Sundays and holidays glad with their joyous voices. And last, but not least, by aid of an elaborate mechanism of hammers, rope, and pulleys, they had for centuries celebrated the departure of every hour with a chorale, and every half-hour with a strain like the versicle of a chant, and every quarter of an hour with a little sprinkle of sweet sound.

Imagine, then, the dismay of the citizens, when, one Monday morning, eight o'clock came, and no sound issued from the cathedral; half-past eight, silence; nine, not a note of warning! Their wonder was increased when the usual peal rung out, clear and full as ever, for the morning service, and by mid-day the whole city was in a commotion. It was plain something must be wrong with the machinery of the chimes.

Immediately the most skilful mechanics of the town, clock-makers and bell-founders, with the men of science, and the whole corporation, in a state-procession, mounted the clock-tower.

"We will soon set it right," they said to the agitated crowd as they entered the belfry-door.

The ropes of the machinery were tested,—all were sound; not a flaw in the hammers; not a clog in the wheels; not a crack in the silvery metal. Microscopes were employed, conjectures were hazarded, experiments of all kinds were tried, but not a ray of light was thrown on the perplexity. The clever hands, and the wise heads, and the will of the authorities were all baffled; and the procession reappeared to the assembled multitudes with very crestfallen looks.

That afternoon little work was done in the workshops, few lessons were learned in the schools, all the routine of household habits was interrupted. And when it grew dark, the Great Square was filled with people who were afraid to separate and go to bed without the sanction of the cathedral chimes. Many foreboded some terrible disaster to the city, and some thought the end of the world was come.

But when it was dark, a sound very weird and strange, yet with a music like the old familiar tones, came from the church-tower, as it rose dim and grand against the starry sky. It was a voice, not human, yet with a strange likeness to a human voice, silvery as a stream, thrilling as a battle-trumpet, familiar to each listener as his own, like the blended voices of a spirit and a bell.

"We have borne it too long," said the bell-voice. "We were set here on high for other purposes than men have put us to. Is not this a cathedral, a sanctuary, and a shrine, sacred with the dust of martyrs, and dedicated to the service of Heaven? Were not we christened like immortals? Were not we consecrated like priests? The touch of holy hands is on us, and shall we be debased to secular uses? Set apart like sacred ministers in a sacred dwelling, shall we be required to mingle in the common circumstances of your daily life? Raised on high to be near the heavens we serve, shall our saintly voices serve to tell you when to eat and sleep?

"We have borne it too long. We will still serve Heaven, and summon you on Sundays and Holydays. We will call you to the solemn services of the Church. We will, if necessary, sound a triumphant peal on days of national thanksgiving, in remembrance of the Victory which first awoke us into music. We will even condescend to ring at your weddings—because marriage is a sacrament—and at your baptisms. We will toll solemnly when your spirits pass from earth, and when your bodies are laid in the churchyard we have seen slowly raised with the dust of your dying generations.

"But henceforth expect us not to do work which your commonest house-clocks can do as well. Let your eight-day clocks—your gilded time-pieces—call you to work, and eat, and rest. We are sacred things, set solemnly apart from all secular uses. Our business is with Eternity, and the Church, and Heaven. Call on us no more to commune with the things of the world, and earth, and time. We are your cathedral bells, but we will be your household clock-chimes no longer."

Then the voice died away on the night air. For a few minutes there was silence, but soon it was broken by sobs and lamentations, and all the people lifted up their voice as one man, and wept.

The house-father said, "Shall we never more hear your voice calling us to morning and evening prayer? Whenever you told us it was the hour, the mother came from her work, and the children from their play, and together we knelt a united family, and committed each other to God."

And the mother said, "Your voices are blended with every happy household time. Sweet bells, will you mingle with our family joys no more? In the morning you wakened us to begin another busy day, and the sun's beams and your voices came together to call us to serve God in our lowly calling; and both, we thought, came to us from heaven; and both, we thought, were meek and lowly, and ready to minister to us in our daily lives, because both were sent from Him who came among us once, not to be ministered unto, but to minister; and both, we thought, had caught something of the light of the eyes which wept at Bethany, and of the tones of the voice which spoke at Cana and at Nain.

"At mid-day you told me it was time to send the dinner to my husband and my elder sons. At six your voice was welcome to us all, because we knew the father's step would soon be on the threshold. At eight you reminded me it was time to lay the little ones to rest, and many a time have you brought happy and holy thoughts to me in those psalms you sang to me whilst I hushed my babes to sleep; and all my everyday life seemed to be more linked with sacred things, to become, as it were, a part of the service of God, because it moved to the music of your voices.

"And again at night your tones were welcome, as in the morning, when they told us the day's work was over, and, wearied, we lay down to peaceful rest. For through the night we knew your sacred voices would sound to Heaven above our sleeping city, like the voices of the angels, who rest not day nor night, saying, Holy, holy, holy. Sweet bells, will you never chime for us again?"

And the children said, in their clear, sweet, ringing voices, "Dear chimes, do not cease to play to us. You wake us to the happy day, you set us free from school, and send us home laughing and dancing for joy; you call our fathers home to us, at night you sing us to sleep, and your voices are blended with our mothers' in our happy dreams. Sweet chimes, you sang so many years to our fathers and mothers; and our grandfathers remember you when they were little children like us. Dear chimes, sing to us still."

And from the sick-chamber, which looked into the cathedral square, where the windows were darkened all day, and sand was strewn before the door, that the din of the passing wheels might jar less roughly on the aching head within, came a low and plaintive voice,—"Sweet bells, your commonest tones are sacred to me. You are my church music, the only church music I can ever hear. When I hear you chime the hour on Sundays and on the festivals, I feel myself among the multitude within your sacred walls, and your voice seems to bear their songs of praise to me, and I am no more alone, but one of the worshippers.

"But at night it is I prize you most. All through the hours

of darkness, so often sleepless to me, your voice is the voice of a friend, familiar as my mother's, yet solemn as the chants of the choir. It helps me to measure off the hours of pain, and say, 'Thank God, an hour less of night, and an hour nearer morning.' And how often, when my suffering is great, you have come with the old psalm-tune, and every tone has brought its word to me, and spoken to me as if direct from God, and filled my heart with trust and peace! Your least sprinkles of sweet sound are precious to me. I fancy they are like the waters of time falling musically from stone to stone on their way to the great sea. I feel they are as the echoes of the footsteps of Him who is drawing nearer and nearer to me, and they draw my heart nearer to Him.

"Sweet bells, your commonest tones are sacred, for what is the world but that which becomes the Church when it learns how God has loved it, and turns from self to Him? And what is Earth but the floor of Heaven, which heavenly feet once trod? And what is Time but the little fragment of Eternity in which we live on earth? Sweet bells, make not my sleepless nights lonely and silent, but sing to me, sing to us all, as of old. Make all our life sacred by linking every fragment of our life to God."

But still no responsive sound came from the cathedral tower, and the people waited on in the silence and the darkness. At last a young priest, an Augustinian friar, ventured a bold suggestion:

"Are not the devils proud, and the angels lowly? Did the angel think it beneath him to say to Elijah, 'Arise, and eat?' Did Gabriel hesitate to descend from the presence of God to bear to an aged priest the tidings of the birth of a child? Did that other angel deem it secular to say to Peter the apostle, 'Gird thyself, and bind on thy sandals, and cast thy garment about thee,' before he led him over the stony streets through the cold night air? And should our cathedral bells scorn to bid us 'rise and eat,' or to chime at our births, or to summon us to 'gird and clothe' ourselves for every day's work? Brethren, proud thoughts, and scorn of daily service, and voices which call our everyday life common and unclean, are not from Heaven. The bells are possessed by a proud and evil spirit. Let us exorcise them."

The suggestion at first startled the people as daring, and irreverent to the church bells, but in their despair, they at length agreed to try it. A solemn procession of priests and holy men and women mounted the cathedral tower, and, in ancient formulas, with prayer and incense, and the music of holy hymns, they exorcised the fiend.

Then at once a tide of pent-up music flowed from the liberated bells. They conscientiously rang out all at once every hour and half-hour they had omitted, and then meekly and steadily resumed their wonted chimes, and continued them ever afterwards, like voices of happy and lowly angels calling men to wake and pray, to "rise and eat," to pray and rest, cheering the workman to his daily labour, and welcoming him from it, chanting to the mother as she lulled her babe, and in the sick-chamber soothing the lonely hours with melodious sound, and waking in the lonely heart sweet echoes of the psalms of praise.

Here the Legend ended. I heard, however, afterwards that the young priest, the Augustinian friar, lived to spread Glad Tidings through the city, but that he was at last burned in the cathedral square for preaching to men what he had said about the church bells. Yet in the flames, it was said, he looked up to the cathedral tower, and sang the words of a psalm of praise the old bells were chiming, till his voice was silenced in death. And ever since, the chimes have taken up his message, and chant to those who will listen, hour by hour.

"'Whether therefore ye eat, or drink, or whatsoever ye do, do all to the glory of God.'"

WHAT MAKES THINGS MUSICAL?

What makes things musical?

"The sun!" said the Forest. "In the night I am still and voiceless. A weight of silence lies upon my heart. If you pass through me, the sound of your own footstep echoes fearfully, like the footfall of a ghost. If you speak to break the spell, the silence closes in on your words, like the ocean on a pebble you throw into it. The wind sighs far-off among the branches, as if he were hushing his breath to listen. If a little bird chirps uneasily in its nest, it is silenced before you can find out whence the sound came.

"But the dawn breaks. Before a gray streak can be seen, my trees feel it, and quiver through every old trunk and tiny twig with joy; my birds feel it, and stir dreamily in their nests, as if they were just murmuring to each other, 'How comfortable we are!'

"Then the wind awakes, and tunes my trees for the concert, striking his hand across one and another, until all their varied harmonies are astir; the soft, liquid rustlings of my oaks and beeches make the rich treble to the deep, plaintive tones of my pines. Then my early birds awake one by one, and answer each other in sweet responses, until the Sun rises, and the whole joyous chorus bursts into song to the organ and flute accompaniments of my evergreens and summer leaves. And in the pauses, countless happy insects chirp, and buzz, and whirl with contented murmuring among my ferns and flower-bells. The Sun makes me musical," said the Forest.

What makes things musical?

"Storms!" said the Sea. "In calm weather I lie still and sleep, or, now and then, say a few quiet words to the beaches I ripple on, or the boats which glide through my waters. But in the tempest you learn what my voice is, when all my slumbering powers awake, and I thunder through the caverns, and rush with all my battle-music on the rocks, whilst, between the grand artillery of my breakers, the wind peals its wild trumpet-peals, and the waters rush back to my breast from the cliffs they have scaled, in torrents and cascades, like the voices of a thousand rivers. My music is battle-music. storms make me musical," said the Sea.

What makes things musical?

"Action!" said the Stream. "I lay still in my mountain-cradle for a long while. It is very silent up there. Occasionally the shadow of an eagle swept across me with a wild cry; but generally, from morning till night, I knew no change save the shadows of my rocky cradle, which went round steadily with the sun, and the shadows of the clouds, which glided across me, without my ever knowing whence or whither. But the rocks and clouds are very silent. The singing-birds did not venture so high; and the insects had nothing to tempt them near me, because no honied flower-bells bent over me there—nothing but little mosses and gray lichens, and these, though very lovely, are quiet creatures, and make no stir.

"I used to find it monotonous sometimes, and longed to have power to wake the hills; and I should have found it more so, had I not felt I was growing, and should flow forth to bless the fields by and by. Every drop that fell into my rocky basin I welcomed. And, at last, the spring rains came, and all my rocks sent me down little rills on every side, and the snows melted into my cup; and, at last, I rose beyond the rim of my dwelling, and was free.

"Then I danced down over the hills, and sang as I went, till all the lonely places were glad with my voice; and I tinkled over the stones like bells, and crept among my cresses like fairy flutes, and dashed over the rocks and plunged into the pools with all my endless harmonies. Action makes me musical," said the Stream.

What makes things musical?

"Suffering!" said the Harp-strings. "We were dull lumps of silver and copper-ore in the mines; and no silence on the living, sunny earth is like the blank of voiceless ages in those dead and sunless depths. But, since then, we have passed through many fires. The hidden earth-fires underneath the mountains first moulded us, millenniums since, to ore; and then, in these last years, human hands have finished the training which makes us what we are.

"We have been smelted in furnaces heated seven times, till all our dross was gone; and then we have been drawn out on the rack, and hammered and fused, and, at last, stretched on these wooden frames, and drawn tighter and tighter, until we wonder at ourselves, and at the gentle hand which strikes such rich and wondrous chords and melodies from us—from us, who were once silent lumps of ore in the silent mines. Fires and blows have done it for us. Suffering has made us musical," said the Harp-strings.

What makes things musical?

"Union!" said the Rocks. "What could be less musical than we, as we rose in bare crags from the hill-tops, or lay strewn about in huge isolated boulders in the valleys? The trees which sprang from our crevices had each its voice; the forests which clothed our sides had all these voices blended in richest harmonies when the wind touched them; the streams which gushed from our stony hearts sang joyous carols to us all day and all night long; the grasses and wild-flowers which clasped their tiny fingers round us had each some sweet murmur of delight as the breezes played with them; but we, who ever thought there was music in us?

"Yet now a human hand has gathered us from moor and mountain and lonely fell, and side by side we lie and give out music to the hand that strikes us. Thus we, who had lain for centuries unconscious that there was a note of music in our hearts, answer one another in melodious tones, and combine in rich chords, just because we have been brought together. Union makes us musical," said the Rocks.

What makes things musical?

"Life!" said the Oak-beam in the good ship. "I know it by its loss. Once I quivered in the forest at the touch of every breeze. Every living leaf of mine had melody, and all together made a stream of many-voiced music; whilst around me were countless living trees like myself, who woke at every dawn to a chorus in the morning breeze. But since the axe was laid at our roots, all the music has gone from our branches. We are useful still, they say, in the gallant ship, and our country mentions us with honour even in death; but the music has gone from us with life for ever, and we can only groan and creak in the storms. Life made us musical," said the Oak-beam.

What makes creatures musical?

"Joy!" laughed the Children, and their happy laughter pealed through the sweet fresh air as they bounded over the fields, as if it had caught the most musical tones of everything musical in nature,—the ripple of waves, the tinkling of brooks, the morning songs of birds. "Joy makes creatures musical," said the Children.

What makes things musical?

"Love!" said the little Thrush, as he warbled to his mate on the spring morning, and the Mother, as she sang soft lullabies to her babe. And all the Creatures said—

"Amen! Love makes us musical. In Storms and Sunshine, Suffering and Joy, Action, Union, Life, Love is the music at the heart of all. Love makes us musical," said all the Creatures.

And from the multitude before the throne, who, through fires of Tribulation and Storms of conflict, had learned the new song, and from depths of Darkness and the silence of Isolation had been brought together in the Light of Life to sing it, floated down a soft "Amen, for God is Love."

THE ACORN

"WHEN will my training begin?" said the acorn to itself, as it unfolded its delicately-carved cup and saucer on the branch of an old oak on the edge of a forest. "I understand I am to be an oak one day, like my father. All the acorns say that is what we are to be, but there certainly seems little chance of it at present. I have been sitting here for no one knows how many days, and I feel no change, except that I look less pretty than I did when I was young and green, and begin to feel rather dry, and shrivelled, and old. At this rate, I do not see much chance of my becoming an oak, or anything else but an old, dry acorn. When will my training begin?"

As it meditated thus, a strong breeze sighed mournfully through the autumn woods, and shook down many brown leaves from the old oak, and with them the acorn.

"This will hinder my progress again," thought the acorn, "for it is evident such a downfall as this can have nothing to do with my education. When will my training begin?"

A day or two afterwards, a drove of hogs was turned into the forest, and they began grunting and grubbing among the dead leaves for acorns. Many of its brethren did our acorn see ruthlessly hurried into those voracious snouts. It kept very quiet under the dead leaves to avoid a similar fate, but it thought—"This is a sad delay. It is too plain that being trampled on and tossed about in this way can teach no one anything. When will my training begin?"

Meanwhile, the swine rummaged among the dead leaves, and trod them under foot, and tossed the decaying mould hither and thither with their snouts and feet, until one of them by accident rolled our acorn down a little hill, where it lay buried under some stray leaves many yards from the edge of the forest, in the outskirts of a park. There it lay unobserved all the rest of the winter.

Even this was a pleasant change after having been tossed about and trodden under foot so long, but in its fall its shrivelled brown skin had cracked, and the acorn thought— "This is a sad disaster. How ever am I to grow into an oak when I am so crushed and cracked that scarcely any one would recognise me for an acorn? When will my training begin?"

All the winter the rain pattered on it, and sank it deeper and deeper under the dead leaves and under the earth-clods, until all its acorn beauty was marred and crushed out of it, and it fell asleep in the dark, under the cold, damp earth; and the snows came and folded it in under their white, eiderdown pillows. At last, the warm touch, that comes to all sleeping nature in the spring, came softly on it, and it awoke.

"What a pity," it said, "I should have lost so much time by falling asleep! I can scarcely make out what I am like, or where I am. What a sad waste of time! It is clear no one can go on with his education in sleep. When will my training begin?"

With these thoughts, it stretched out two little green things on each side of it, which felt like wings; and tried to peep out of its hole. And, to its delight, it succeeded, and, with a few more efforts, even contrived to keep its head steadily above ground, and look around it.

"There is my father, the old oak," it said. "He looks quite green again. But I am a long way off from him, and how very small and close to the ground! When shall I begin to be like him?"

But meantime it was very happy. It felt so full of life, although so small; and the sun shone so graciously on it, and all the showers and dews seemed so full of kindly desires to help and nourish it. And more and more little green leaves expanded from its sides, and more and snore little busy roots shot down into the earth, and the leaves breathed and drank in the sunshine, and the roots were great chemists and cooks, and concocted a perpetual feast for it out of the earth and stones.

But it thought sometimes, "This is all exceedingly pleasant, and I am very happy; but, of course, this is not education; it is only enjoying myself. When will my training begin?"

The next spring, the early frosts had much more power over it in its detached, exposed situation than over the saplings in the shelter of the forest. And it saw the trees in the wood growing green, and tempting the song-birds beneath their leafy tents, whilst the sap still flowed feebly upward through its tiny cells, and its twigs and leaf-buds were still brown and hard.

"This must be a great hindrance to me," it thought—"this, no doubt, will retard my education considerably. What a pity I stand here so detached and unprotected! When will my training begin?"

But in the late spring came some days of black east wind and bitter frost, and it saw the more forward leaves in the wood turn pale and shrivel before they unfolded, and then fall off; nipped and lifeless, to join the old dead leaves of the past autumn, whilst its own little buds lay safe within their hard and glossy casings, protected by one enemy against a worse. And when the east wind and the black frosts were gone, the little sapling shot up freely.

In that summer, and the next, and the next, it made great progress. But in the fourth autumn, a great disappointment awaited it. The owner of the park in which it grew came by, and stood beside it, and said to his forester—

"That sapling is worth preserving, it is so vigorous and healthy; and, standing in this detached position, it will break the line of the wood, and look well from my house. We will watch it, and set a fence around it to guard it from the cattle. But it has thrown out a false leader. Take your knife and cut this straggling shoot away, and next year, I have no doubt, it will grow well."

Then the forester applied his knife carefully to the false leader, and cut it off. But the sapling, not having understood the master's words, nor observed with what care and design the knife was applied, felt wounded to the core.

"My best and strongest shoot," it sighed to itself. "It was a cruel cut. It will take me a long time to repair that loss. T am afraid it has lost me at least a year. When will my training begin?"

But the next year the master's words were fulfilled.

Thus years passed on. And slowly, twig by twig, and shoot by shoot, the sapling grew. Sunbeams expanded its leaves; rains nourished its roots; frosts, checking its early buds, hardened its wood; winds swaying it hither and thither, as if they were determined to level it, only rooted it more firmly. And year by year the top grew a little higher, and the wood a little firmer, and the trunk a little thicker, and the roots a little deeper; but so slowly, that summer by summer it said—

"This is very pleasant; but it is only breathing, and being happy. It certainly cannot be the discipline which forms the great oaks. When will my training begin?"

And autumn by autumn, as the sap flowed downward, and the buds ceased to expand, and the branches grew leafless and dry, it thought—

"This is a sad loss of time. Now I am falling into torpor again, and shall make not an inch of progress for six long months. When will my training begin?"

And winter by winter, as the winds bent it to and fro, and made its branches creak, and threatened its very existence, and the heavy snows sometimes broke its boughs—

"These are sore trials. I may be thankful if I barely struggle through them! In days like these existence is an effort, and endurance the utmost one can attain. When will my training begin?"

And in the spring, when the frosts nipped its finest buds—

"These little nips and checks are very annoying; but one must bear them patiently. They are certainly hindrances; and it is disheartening, when one does one's best, to be continually thrown back by these trifling checks. When will my training begin?"

But, one summer day, a little girl and an old man came and seated themselves under its shade. By this time it had seen some generations of men, and had learned something of human language.

The old man said—"I remember, when I was a very little boy, my grandfather telling me how, when he was young, he had marked this tree, then a mere sapling, and pruned it of a false shoot, which would have spoiled its beauty, and had it fenced and preserved. And now my little grand-daughter and I sit under its shade! The fence has long since decayed; but it is not needed. The cattle come and lie under its shadow, as we do. It is a noble oak-tree now, and gives shelter instead of needing it."

Then the oak rustled above them; and the old man and the child thought it was a summer breeze stirring the branches. But in reality it was the oak laughing to itself, as it thought—

"Then I am really a tree! And, whilst I was wondering when my training would begin, it has been finished, and I am an oak after all!"

PARABLES IN HOUSEHOLD THINGS

THE sick girl lay in her shaded room, in the street of a great city, and thought, "If I could only leave this prison of mine, and look at the beautiful world, I know I should grow happier and holier with every breath I drew. The thorny bud on the brown branches in spring would give me promise of resurrection; every butterfly would tell me of life through death; every flower would lift my heart to Him who cares for our little pleasures; every bubbling spring would murmur to me of the living water; every corn-field and garden would repeat the sacred parables. But here I can see nothing of God's making but the sky, and that is too high and far. I want some steps to take my feeble thoughts gently up to heaven. But around me are only manufactured things, which speak to me only of earth, and time, and man."

She leant back listlessly on her couch. Twilight came over the room, the glowing coals stirred quietly as they burnt away, and then it seemed as if an angel's hand touched her ears and opened them, for the dark and silent room became full of soft and soothing harmonics. All the mute and inanimate things about her found voices and spoke comfort to her heart.

Together they said—"It is true we are only manufactured things; but do not despise us for that! We came originally, as much as you yourself, or the flowers, and the trees, and the sunbeams, from one Divine Hand. It is only that we have been trained and moulded by human hands to be what we are. And just so are you; God creates you, but life moulds you. Your trial and your training come like ours, mostly through human hands, although you are destined for higher plans and more blessed services. Listen to us, for we have messages for you, each one of us."

Then the stones from the wall said—"We come from the mountains far away, from the sides of the craggy hills. Fire and water worked on us for ages, but only made us crags. Human hands have made us into a dwelling where the children of your immortal race are born, and suffer, and rejoice, and find rest and shelter, and learn the lessons set them by our Maker and yours. But we have passed through much to fit us for this. Gunpowder has rent our very heart; pickaxes have cleaved and broken us, it seemed to us often without design or meaning, as we lay misshapen stones in the quarry; but gradually we were cut into blocks, and some of us were chiselled with finer instruments to a sharper edge. But we are complete now, and are in our places, and are of service. You are in the quarry still, and not complete, and therefore to you, as once to us, much is inexplicable. But you are destined for a higher building, and one day you will be placed in it by hands not human; a living stone in a heavenly temple."

Then the glass water-beaker said—"I was hard flint and waste sand on the desolate sea-shore once, but human hands gathered me, and fused me in furnaces heated seven times, and took me out to let me cool, and cast me in again, and shaped and cut me till at last I carry your water from the spring, and am pressed with many a thankful glance to your parched lips. I am complete. But you, when you have passed through your fires, will be a vessel of living water in a better hand, and bear many a draught of refreshment to weary and thirsty hearts."

"I also have been in many furnaces," said the china flower-vase. "The colours you so often admire in me, have been burnt in slowly, stage by stage, every fresh colour requiring a fresh fusing in the furnace. But you, when your trial is over, shall carry flowers of Paradise and leaves from the tree of life for the healing of the nations."

"And I," said the clock, "am scarcely an individual being. I am a little world in myself—a wondrous combination of mechanism. Each of my wheels and springs, with my unwearied pendulum, has its own history of fires and blows and ruthless instruments. None of us could form the slightest idea, as we lay dismembered in our various workshops, what we were designed for. Only in combination with every other part, has any part of us any meaning. You are not a little world like me, but a fragment of a great world. When all that belong to you are gathered together, you will understand it all as we do now. And your voice will mark with joyous music the flight of blessed ages which only lead to others more and more blessed throughout eternity."

"And I," said the bronze pastille-burner, "came from ages of darkness in the depths of the earth. Human hands brought me to the light, moulded and sculptured me, and set me here to burn sweet perfumes, and diffuse fragrance around me. But you will be an incense-bearer in a Temple by and by, and from you shall stream a fragrance of love and praise acceptable to God."

"The quarries were my birthplace also," said the alabaster night-lamp; "but you shall be a light-bearer, when your training is complete, of a light which is life, and which has no need of night, like my dim flame, to make it visible."

"I," sang the guitar, with the wooden frame and metallic strings, "am a twofold being. I lived and waved in the forest once; and then the woodman's axe was laid on me, and I fell,—I fell, and the life departed from me; and from a living, life-bearing tree, I became mere inanimate timber. More blows, more tearing with saws, more sharp cutting with knife and chisel, and I became melodious again, simply from being united with these metallic strings, which never had life, but lay silent in mines, till the hand of man woke them into music. And thus together we respond to your gentle touch, and soothe for you many a lonely hour. Life from death, music through fires of trial: this is also your destiny. Hereafter every nerve of your tried and perfected being shall respond to the slightest touch of the Hand you love, filling heaven with happy music."

"As for me," said the pages of the hymn-book, "my discipline has, perhaps, been the severest of all. Once rustling in the flax-field, rejoicing in the dews and sunshine, I was torn, racked, twisted, and woven by many iron hands into linen. Then, for a time, treated carefully, decorated and treasured, and washed and perfumed, I was afterwards thrown scornfully away. Yet, even in that low estate, I found comfort. Even as a rag I bound up the wounds of suffering soldiers in a military hospital. But I was to sink lower yet. I was thrown into a mill, and pounded, crushed, and torn, till I was a mere shapeless pulp. Yet from those depths, my true life began. Process after process succeeded, till here, at last,

I am to speak to you undying words of hope and love. And you also, one day, shall shine forth a living epistle, proclaiming to angels and men for ever and for ever such words as speak to you from my pages now!"

The sick girl smiled, and was comforted. "Yet," she said, "the fires are fierce, the blows are heavy, the trial is long. The end is, indeed, well worth them all; but sometimes the end seems distant!"

"Yes," responded the hymn-book; "my history resembles yours in one happy feature more than that of any of us besides. For even in your days of training you are of service. You may clothe cold limbs, and bind up many wounds even now, as I did when I was a poor linen-rag. And, more than that, even now, in your time of trial, the ministries you are destined for at last may be begun. Even now you may be a living epistle, a book wherein many may read lessons of hope and patience, and sing praises, as they look on you, as you do when you look on me."

"Yes," responded the stones; "even now you are a living stone. The temple you are to form is building even now."

And the pastille-burner:—"Even now your prayers and praises may rise like sweet incense."

And the water-glass:—"Many a draught of living water may you carry, even now, in the dry and thirsty land, to hearts that need it."

And the night-lamp:—"Even now in the night, thou, child of the day, sheddest light around thee—a little light, it may be, in a narrow circle, yet which, though thou mayest not know it, cheers and guides not a few, even now."

And the guitar:—"Many a strain of thankful song has come from the depths of your heart, even now, in these your days of trial, to blend with my harmonies, and to soar to regions which my poor metallic music can never reach!"

And all the mute things sang together—"We are complete and rejoice to serve you, vessels meet for your using. One day you also shall be perfected, a vessel meet for the Master's use. And then He will take you into His house, unto the temple which is a home and your home for ever. Like us, when you are perfected, you shall serve; but, unlike us, even whilst you are being perfected, you may serve!"

Then the sufferer turned over the leaves of another Book, and saw how the Master had written His parables, not in streams, and corn-fields, and birds, and flowers, and fruitful earth, and starry sky alone, but in common household things, and common human ties. And henceforth, not nature only, but everyday cares, and duties, and relationships, and all things around her, became for her illuminated with the lessons of His love.

PASSAGES FROM THE LIFE OF A FERN

MY life has been one of such extraordinary vicissitudes as might have made many almost doubt their own identity. But it is only to-day that I have learned its real purpose. To-day, for the first time, I am content. A light has dawned on me which makes all the dark passages of my former life clear and luminous, and unites the whole into one harmonious picture. I will narrate a few of my adventures to you while I am full of this happy discovery.

The first thing I can remember is being in a world overflowing with life in every form. It was a tropical forest. Gigantic palms rose above me so high that I could not see their feathery crowns. From one erect stem to another hung tangled festoons of parasites and climbing plants, broad, rich, green leaves which fell into stately crowns with their own weight, enormous gorgeous flowers, delicate wreaths of intertwined many-coloured blossoms and many-shaped foliage; so that when I looked up, I could scarcely see one point of the deep blue sky, except when a strong wind made rifts in my fretted roof. Scarcely one ray of light fell on me pure, but broken and green and tremulous, softly shaded, or tinted like a rainbow through the flowers.

The animals which lived in our forest depths I cannot distinctly recall. I have not seen any like them for so many thousand years. But all was gigantic, and many would seem misshapen monsters to us now. Yet then it was quite natural, and an everyday thing, to hear the great tree-eaters tramping each like an army through the forest shades, cropping the tops of the highest trees, and devouring branches as our animals crop the herbage. Trees crackled under them like brambles.

We dreaded much, we smaller creatures, to see these approach, for they trampled down a generation of us under the tread of their ponderous feet. There were lizards whose scales glittered like the waves of the sea in the sunshine, each scale a massive prismatic metallic plate. And from the lower reaches of the forest, where the hot mist steamed up from the marshy hollows, monstrous creatures, half-fish, half-forest-climbers, occasionally strayed among us.

I cannot recall if there was music in the forest; yet I think I hear across these countless years the dim echoes of strange voices, which have been silenced for ages on the earth, a confusion of wild calls and cries in the mornings and evenings, weird bell-notes tolling through the sultry noon-day silences, and a confused whirr, and buzzing, and croaking, and whizzing, and rustling of countless smaller animals which have perished and left no trace of their existence behind.

But the creatures which impressed the restless character on my being, which only to-day the sun has smiled away, were some near relations of my own. For, although I was but a little fern, many of my race were among the lords of the forest. Their roots spread into magnificent curved pedestals; their stems rose, decorated, and erect as the palms, to the height of the tallest trees; and their fronds expanded into ribbed and fretted roofs, beneath which hundreds like me could find shade and shelter, yet every frond as delicately fringed and edged as any of ours.

I thought—"These are my elder sisters. One day I shall grow like them."

Thus my own daily life seemed empty and shadowy to me, because of the strong yearning that possessed me to be great like them. It did not make me discontented or desponding, but filled me with a wild and feverish expectation which made the present appear nothing to me. I stretched out my little fronds, and caught every sunbeam and rain-drop I could; and when a shower came, and the life-giving waters circulated through my veins, I throbbed with vague desire, and thought, "Now I am to be something."

But with all my efforts, I never could grow to be any thing but a little fern! So the summer passed, and then I felt myself growing shrivelled and old. My limbs contracted, my fronds curled up and turned dry and brown, and in a few weeks I was scarcely visible. But the spring revived me and my yearnings, and I grew certainly very handsome and tall for one of my branch of our family; but still only a little fern!

The forest decayed, I know not how. The marsh extended, and, instead of the world of varied exuberant life, we lay a long time a mass of steaming, mouldering decay. And then, through millenniums more, we stiffened and hardened and grew black and shapeless, and were buried in the dark, no one can say how long, for to us, throughout those changeless ages, there were no days and no seasons to measure time.

At last a light came to us, not the sun, but a little trembling light, in the hands of a living creature, such as we had never seen. I know now it was a man. Then followed a time of stir and noise and knocking about, such as I shall never forget. We were hewn with pickaxes, and tossed into buckets, and, at last, lifted into the real old sunlight we had not seen for countless ages. The sun was the same as ever, as young and bright, it seemed, as he had been thousands of years before; but we did not bask long in his beams.

A period followed of darkness and cold and silence, in which all the world seemed to have forgotten my existence, although I had been dragged out of my native bed, and stored in this den with so much pains. But they remembered us at last.

One evening, after passing through a great deal of commotion, I found myself in an open place, with many of my brethren. A light like that we had first seen, after our ages of darkness in the heart of the earth, was applied to us, and then the strangest transformation passed over me.

Just as the water had streamed through my green veins in the forest of old, a new element began to course through all my black and stony heart. That light ran through and through me, until I became, not a receiver, but actually a giver of light. Instead of my green fronds, delicate pencils of red and golden flame streamed from me, until I became one glowing substance; and, in my own light, I actually saw living faces looking thankfully at me, and human hands stretched out to feel my warmth, just as of old I had spread my fronds in the rays of the sun.

But I was too full of my old vague longings to enjoy or observe any of those things much, for I thought, with glowing confidence, "Now, I am to be something great at last!"

It was the last glimmer of that vague ambition in me. My light faded, I grew cold, and, which was worse, I fell to pieces, became mere dust, and was wafted about by the slightest breath, so that I had the greatest difficulty in preserving my own identity. I was even ignominiously swept away by the very hands which had spread so gratefully in my light only a few hours before, and tossed contemptuously out into a rubbish heap behind the house.

But there, happily for me, I was once more in the sunshine; and the sun, and all heavenly creatures, think scorn of no one. They smiled on me, a poor heap of ashes, as if I had been a tree-fern; and the gentle dews descended on me, as if had been a flower; and the birds and winds scattered seeds amongst us, until I began to feel once more something like the stirrings of life within me. I had blended my being with a little seed, and in the spring, green tufts of life burst out from my shrivelled heart. I grew, and spread, and drank in rain and sunshine, until at length I waved and expanded in the summer breeze—a little fern!

Then a bright, transforming thought flashed through me. In the tropical forest, in the black coal-beds, on the glowing hearth, I had not been an imperfect likeness and a vague promise of something else, but myself, in my little degree, pleasant and serviceable; exactly the best thing it was possible for me to be, filling up my tiny measure of service in the world, so that the world would have been the poorer for that tiny measure of pleasure and good without me. How happy I might have been always, if I had known this before! How happy I am to know it now!

I begin life again, but I have learned my lesson. I am something; not something great, but something I was meant to be—a little green happy fern. At this moment I tremble with joy in the soft breezes, I thrill with life, I drink the rain-drops, and the next moment and to-morrow will bring each its store of work and joy for me, and I shall be the highest thing I could wish to be, the thing I was made to be. And now I am here near the tall trees, and among the many-coloured flowers, a little, happy, lowly fern.

PARABLES

THE CLOCK-BELL AND THE ALARM-BELL

"WE have lived a long time here together," said the ponderous Alarm-bell to the little brisk bell in the clock-tower of the Orphan-house, "and a useful life yours has been! I have watched carefully, and never once during these hundred years that we have stood side by side have you failed to tell the hours and half-hours by day and night. I have plenty of leisure for thought; but it would be beyond my powers to calculate how often your voice has been heard in the service of man.

"I observe, too, how much attention is paid you by all, and with how much well-deserved respect you are regarded. Nothing is done in house or field without your sanction. At your early call, this little busy hive begins to stir in the morning. At your mid-day invitation, the boys gather from the fields where they have been working; and the girls from the laundries and workrooms to the noon-day meal. At your evening summons, the doors are closed at night, and not a sound is heard afterwards in house or field until your steady voice wakens our little world again.

"Yours is, indeed, a useful, honoured life; but as for me, who can tell what I am made for? Since I was placed here first, a hundred years ago, lifted up with enormous trouble and labour, and safely roofed in my belfry, not a creature has heard my voice, or been the better for my existence. I might as well have been lying still a lump of unsmelted ore in the depths of the mines. I feel so stiff and rusty, that I sometimes question if they could move me if they tried.

"For you, daily, hourly usefulness! For me, a hundred years of silence! And who can say how many more? I do not complain; but our destinies are very different. It must be wonderfully happy to be so useful, and to be looked on by everyone with such attention and regard. Of course, I could not expect to be as serviceable as you—I, with my cumbrous, ponderous mass of heavy metal, and you, hung so lightly, so graceful in your shape, so brisk in all your movements, so cheery and pleasant in your voice. But I should like to be of some use once in my life, even if it were only to know for what purpose I was made, and set on high."

"Wait!" said the Clock-bell. "There must be some work for you. It would have taken a hundred such as I am to make one like you. Think of the trouble there must have been in getting a mould large enough for you—of the labour it was to raise you so high. You must be set there for some end, although we do not yet know what. Wait!" said the Clock-bell, cheerily, and struck nine.

Then there was a sound from within the house, as of many childish voices singing an evening hymn. A few minutes after, all was still, and ten o'clock echoed over the silent fields to the sleeping city near at hand.

But that night there was an unusual stir in the Orphan-house. Feet were heard rushing hither and thither; and from every window poured forth the cry: "Fire! Fire! The Orphan-house is on fire!"

And, through the darkness, lurid smoke began to rise from an outhouse attached to the main building.

Then came another cry: "The Alarm-bell! Ring the Alarm-bell!"

And feet were heard on the steps of the belfry-tower; and hands began pulling vigorously at the ropes, and in a moment, for the first time, the deep tones of the long silent bell pealed heavily on the midnight air. They awoke the city. In a short time, fire-engines were on the way. Streams of water played on the flames, and quenched them; and the children and the Orphan-house were saved.

The next morning all was silent again, as if nothing had happened; the outhouse lay in ashes, but the Orphan-house was uninjured. At eight the Clock-bell called the children to their morning prayer; whilst the Alarm-bell had relapsed into silence, perhaps for another century.

But the Clock-bell said—"You have done in an hour the service of a century. Had it not been for you, I should never have struck another hour."

And the grateful children often looked up as they passed

beneath, and said—"Had it not been for our good Alarm-bell, we might all have perished!"

So the Alarm-bell learned what it was made for; and was content to wait another hundred years, or more, before its voice was heard again.

THORNS AND SPINES[1]

IN a garden there once grew a beautiful, blossoming thorn. When the spring came, for a fortnight it was always clothed with a robe of white blossoms. They seemed at once relics of winter, and promises of summer. It was as if Winter, in departing from the earth, had left behind a fragment of his snowy vestments; and Spring, touching them with her magic wand, had transformed them from snow-wreaths into wreaths of snowy blossoms. They were beautiful even in fading; and for many days after the whiteness had gone, they glowed into a delicate pink, and strewed the earth with silky petals when they fell.

On this thorn, one spring, a little brown leaf-bud formed, at the foot of a green twig, the cradle of the green twigs of the next spring. But it happened that, as this brown leaf-bud watched the beauty of the flowers, it grew discontented with its destiny:—

"Why am not I a flower-bud?" it murmured, inside its little brown casing. "That would be worth living for!—To fill the air with delicate fragrance, to be sung to by the birds, to be gathered by human hands as a treasure; or even to live unnoticed by any one, but only to be a flower!—A beautiful, fragrant creature, with a coat of many colours, and a crown of golden stamens, and with promise in its heart;—that would be worth living for! But to be a leaf-bud, a brown, dark, hard leaf-bud!—It would be better to die at once."

And a discontented shiver ran through its veins; and all that summer it never cared to drink in sun or rain, but sat and shivered, and shrivelled on its stem, while all around it, meek and happy buds were growing strong and full of life, nourished by the same rain and sunshine. And in the spring, when the white shower of snowy flowers came again on the

---

[1] Thorns are abortive leaf-buds. Spines are the lower leaves of plants metamorphosed into bristles, to guard the young tree from the attacks of cattle. This little parable was suggested by a passage in "Modern Painters."

thorn-tree, and the other leaf-buds had expanded into green twigs, waving and whispering in the breeze, with each a new bud at its feet, the envious and discontented bud had shrivelled and narrowed itself into a thorn, which pierced the hand of the child, as it reached up to gather the spray of fair white blossom.

*   *   *   *

In a field near this garden, there grew a green shrub, which at the top expanded into luxuriant branches, giving shade at mid-day to man and beast. But from the lower branches, instead of broad green leaves, grew long sharp spines. One summer day, these spines said to each other, in their short and broken speech, for they could not wave and rustle in the wind like the leaves:—

"We are not worthy to live on the same tree with the beautiful forest leaves which wave in the fresh air above us. We can make no refreshing sound as they do; we give no shade as they do to any creature; and we only prick any one that tries to touch us. But it is very pleasant to us to be allowed to grow from the same trunk as they; and it is very kind of the sweet leaves to sing to us as if we belonged to them, and not to be ashamed of us. We are certainly most happily situated; so far beyond what we have any right to expect!"

But all the leaves rustled in a joyous chorus, and said:—
"You are our elder sisters, meek and useful spines! If it had not been for you, we should never have come into life at all, and man and beast would have had no shade from us. The hungry cattle would have eaten us before we unfolded, and our parent-tree would never have grown to what it is, had it not been for you, our faithful and patient guardians. If you had rebelled against the gracious hand that moulds us all, and prevented our expanding into leaves, we should all have perished together long ago. We owe our life to you!" murmured the leaves.

And the rough spines quivered through all their faithful hearts at the words of the leaves.

Then the master passed by, and he said:—"Well done, my faithful spines! You have done your work, and guarded my treasures well. But for you, my trees would have had no leaves, and my fields no shade."

And the spines wondered, and rejoiced greatly; for they had never thought that, in meekly and contentedly bearing their rough lot, and being what they were meant to be, they were serving the master, and doing such good work for others.

SUNSHINE, DAYLIGHT, AND THE ROCK[2]

SUNSHINE and Daylight had one day a serious difference of opinion about a rocky waste, over which their course led them.

"I am not severe," said Daylight, fixing her clear, generalising gray eyes on the Rock. "If I cannot, like some people, see nothing but what I wish to see, no one ever accused me of blackening any one's character. I have known that old rock more years than I care to mention; not a jagged edge, nor a whimsical cranny, but I am intimately acquainted with, and I do not hesitate to say, that a more barren, unmitigated rock I seldom meet with. I do not slander it. I only say, it is nothing more or less than a rock."

Sunshine said nothing, but peeped round the shoulder of her cousin's gray cloak, until the smile of her soft eye met the eye of a little blue violet, which, by dint of hard living, had contrived to obtain a secure footing in a crevice of the old rock; and a flutter of joy passed through the blossoms and leaves of the violet, and communicated itself to a tuft of dry short grass, which had ensconced itself behind. The red and gray cups of some tiny moss and lichens, which had crept into corners here and there, next drank in her kind glances, and fancied themselves wine-cups at a feast. Here and there specks of colour and points of life revealed themselves, and, as they looked, expanded.

By this time, Sunshine had folded Daylight to sleep on her warm breast. Many weeks had passed, when, one quiet afternoon, Daylight again came that way, and glancing critically around, she murmured to Sunshine, "Where is the old gray rock you were so sanguine about?"

Sunshine was silent: her motto being, "Not 'in word, neither in tongue; but in deed and in truth.'"

And at length, Daylight's quiet eyes awoke to the fact, that the grassy knoll where flowers—tiny rock-plants indeed, but still flowers—and mosses lay dozing unawakened by her

---

[2] * Reprinted from "Excelsior."

sober tread, was none other than the rock she had known of old. And she said, meekly, "Truly I find that one way to create beauty is to perceive it."

Then an angel, who was hovering near, on his way back from some message of mercy (for the angels never linger till their messages are given), sang softly, "Love veileth a multitude of sins."

And the old Rock answered in a chorus, through its moss-threads, and lichen-cups, and leaves, and blossoms, "And under the warm veil spring a multitude of flowers."

Wanderers and Pilgrims

A LARGE tract of country lay spread before me; upland and lowland, hill and plain. The whole land seemed stirring with perpetual movement, all in one direction;—from the bright hills at its commencement, to the dark mountains at the end. Earth and sky seemed moving, as when an enormous flight of migratory birds is passing by, but earth and sky were really stationary. This movement was one constant tide of human life, ceaselessly streaming across the land.

It began on a range of wooded hills, with their sunny southern slopes, forests and flowery banks, and grassy and golden fields. Down these slopes, joyous bands ran fast. As I looked closer, I saw the movement was not incessant in the case of each individual; only the ceaseless passing of the great tide of life made it seem so. Merry groups paused on the hill-sides, and made fairy gardens, and twined leafy tents where they would sit a little while and sing and dance. But only a little while! No hand seemed driving them on; it appeared only an inward irresistible instinct. Yet soon the bright groups were scattered, and moved down again over the hills, often never joining more.

"Why do you hasten away from these sunny slopes?" I said. "There seems nothing so pleasant in all the land besides."

"Perhaps not," the travellers replied, with a slight sigh; but it ended in a snatch of song as they danced gaily on. "Perhaps not, but we are a race of Wanderers! We cannot stay; and perhaps better things await us in the plain."

"Whither are you going?" I asked.

"We know not," was the answer; "only onward, onward!"

In the plain were buildings of more solid construction, houses and cities. And here I observed many of the travellers would have gladly lingered, but it could not be. Homesteads, and corn-fields, and vineyards, all had to be left; and still the tide of life streamed on and on.

"Why?" I asked.

"It is the doom of our race," they said, sorrowfully; "we are a people of Wanderers."

"Whither?" I inquired.

"We do not know," was the reply; "only onwards and onwards to the dark mountains!"

Slower and slower grew the footsteps of the Wanderers, more and more regretful the glances they cast behind. Slower, yet with fewer pauses. The strange restless impulse drove them steadily on, until, wearied and tottering, they began the ascent of the dark mountains.

"What is on the other side?" I asked.

"The sea," they said, "the Great Sea."

"How will you cross it, and what is beyond?"

"We know not," they said, with bitter tears. "But we are a doomed race of Wanderers—onwards, onwards; we may not stay!"

Then first I perceived that, among these multitudes of aimless Wanderers, there was one band who kept close together, and moved with a freedom and a purpose, as if they journeyed on not from a blind, irresistible impulse, but from choice. Their looks were seldom turned regretfully behind them, or only on the dark mountains. They looked to something higher.

I asked them—"Why are you thus hasting on?"

"We are Pilgrims," they replied; "we would not linger here."

"Whither are you going?" I inquired.

"Home!" they answered, joyfully. "To a Holy City which is our Home."

"But how do you know the way?" I asked, for no barriers seemed to limit their path, so that any of the Wanderers might join it at any point.

"We know it by two marks," they answered—"by the footsteps of One who trod it once, and left indelible footprints wherever He stepped. And we know it also by the goal to which it tends!"

Then looking up, I saw resting on the mountains where this path ended, a bridge like a rainbow, and beyond it, in the sky, a range of towers and walls, pearl and opal, ruby and golden, such as in a summer evening is sometimes faintly pictured on the clouds, when the setting sun shines through them.

And the little band chanted as they went, "The doom of our race is reversed for us. We are not Wanderers; we are Pilgrims. We would not linger here; this is not our rest. Onwards, upwards, to the City!—To the Home!"

THE ARK AND THE FORTRESS

ONE day, I had been thinking about the terrors of the Great Flood, when it seemed to me that I saw back through the long ages to that distant day, as you look with a night-glass through the night to an illuminated planet.

I saw an old man, venerable with the centuries by which we count the lives of nations, not of men, yet vigorous with the vitality of one who had still centuries to live. He stood on an inland plain, far from any sea; yet above him rose the sides of a large ship. It had been finished that day.

Once more the old man warned the laughing crowds around of the waters which would surely come and float the vessel high above the submerged world. He had told them the same truth for a hundred and twenty years. There had been no indefiniteness about his prophecy. As, since then, men have been warned by the uncertainty of a doom which may come at any moment; then, they were warned by the certainty of a period definitely fixed. Every fall of the leaf had brought it precisely a year nearer. And now the last evening of the last year had come, and once more the patient preacher of righteousness stood and warned them to forsake the sin which must bring the doom.

But in vain. There was no persecution; perhaps some mockery, as they pointed to the cloudless sky, and the fields and forests growing daily greener in the spring-tide sunshine; but for the most part simply unbelief and indifference. "They ate, they drank, they married, they were given in marriage." And so the last warning was finished, and the last evening closed.

But one little group seemed to me to detach itself from the rest with a bolder confidence. They pointed to a fortress on the highest summit of the mountain range above them, and said:—

"If what you say is true, surely we shall be safer there than in a floating ark like yours. In the rushing of the great water-floods you speak of, and the beating of the storms, our mountain fortress will serve us better, at least, than your wooden walls. We shall look down from our height on your waters, and, perchance, see the wreck of your vessel drifted to our feet!"

The patriarch and his family were shut in the ark. Before the next morning, the day of doom had set in. Not a break in the pitiless roof of clouds. Steadily the torrents poured from the opened flood-gates of heaven, whilst the waters from beneath broke their barriers, and the reservoirs under the hills burst forth in sudden rivers.

The flood had begun. The valleys became lakes, the plains seas; but the builders of the mountain fortress had fled to it, and looked triumphantly down on the waves.

Higher and higher they rose. The lower hills were covered. The mountain range was isolated. But the dwellers in the fortress thought, "We are well provisioned. This cannot last for ever!"

The waters rose. Peak after peak became an island. And at last, the highest peak, on which the fortress stood, looked out alone upon the waste of waters, and the floating ark buoyed up securely on them.

They looked still down on the waters, but with trembling hearts. The wild waves dashed furiously against this one remaining obstacle. The firmest human masonry cannot stand like the everlasting rocks. The strong foundations gave way, and with a crash, and a wail of anguish, the fortress fell, and nothing rose above the waters but the floating ark. For nothing that is founded on earth can escape the doom of earth. But—

"Planted Paradise was not so firm
 As was, and is, Thy floating ark."

THE THREE DREAMS

I HAD once three dreams in close succession, which I will relate to you.

In the first, I saw a magnificent palace, a little world of gardens and buildings, a city in itself. All was enclosed within a high wall, so that from outside you could see nothing of it except the fairy white minarets, pencilled delicately against the blue sky, some lofty battlemented watch-towers, and several graceful campaniles, with the tops of a few of the highest trees. But a delicious blending of the fragrance of a thousand flowers came thence in summer evenings; and every night, bell-tower, watch-tower, spire, and dome, and minaret were illuminated with innumerable starry lamps, as if every day within the palace were a festival.

Around the palace were the lanes and alleys of the city— scenes of poverty and squalor—which contrasted strangely with it; and wretched, half-starved-looking creatures, with tattered garments and faces worn with deep marks of want and woe, lingered round the gates. Outside the gates!—and this was one strange incongruity of my dream, for on the gates were emblazoned in golden letters, which were illuminated into transparencies at night, the words—

"Knock, and it shall be opened unto you."

The gates were solid, and enormously massive, like blocks of black marble. No violence could have forced them. There was no crevice at which any one could get a glimpse of what was within. But the golden knocker, underneath those golden words, was so low as to be within reach of the youngest children. Indeed, I noticed that none tried it so often as little children; and whenever any one knocked with the very feeblest sound, in time, and often immediately, the stately portals opened from within, turning on their massive hinges with a sound like the music of many choirs, and the applicant was quietly drawn inside.

Then I saw that the inside of the gates was of translucent

pearl. A stream of light and fragrance for a moment came through, and induced others afterwards to knock. But immediately the gates were closed, and stood a wall of impenetrable marble as before.

I awoke, and whilst meditating on my dream fell asleep again.

In my second dream, I saw the same palace as in my first, but the massive doors were gone, and in their place stood the form of One whom, although I had never seen Him, I had heard so often described, and so faithfully, by those who had seen Him, that I knew Him at once. The same wretched beings were cowering round; but the massive barriers were gone, and in their place He stood, and said, in tones that every one could hear—

"'I am the Door: by me if any man enter in, he shall be saved.'"

One wretched and woe-worn woman gave a trembling glance at His face, and then listening again to those tones, not welcoming merely, but pleading and persuasively tender, she ventured close to Him, and fell on her knees to kiss the hem of His garment.

But He stooped, and stretched out His hand, and took her hand, and led her in.

Then I understood what His words had meant;—that by saying, "I am the door," He must have meant that there was no barrier, no impenetrable gate, but that in the doorway, where the door had been, He stood, and, instead of the lifeless knocker, stretched out His living hands to aid and welcome all who came.

And I awoke from my second dream.

*   *   *   *

Before long I fell asleep again, and then again I saw the same palace, with the massive portals flung open wide, but that gracious princely form stood in them no more. Among the most wretched of that crowd He went—among the maimed, the halt, and the blind.

They thronged around Him, yet many of them scarcely seemed to heed, they were so intent on their own sordid pursuits. Some were crowding with sharp, eager faces round a rag merchant, bargaining with the most absorbing passion for his wretched wares, and then separating to quarrel and fight over their purchases, or bartering their rags again as eagerly for a draught of the intoxicating drinks which had made so many of them the lost creatures they were. Not a rag or a burning drop was to be had except for money, and often for a price which to them was life itself.

And He came to them from the palace, and offered them the palace freely, yet few listened. But with that strange absence of the sense of incongruity and the emotion of surprise characteristic of dreams, I did not wonder! Patiently He went in and out among them, pleading with one and another, often encountering rough words and blows; yet still His words were—

"I come to seek and to save that which was lost."

And some even of the most wretched listened, and returned with Him, and were welcomed inside.

As if "Knock, and it shall be opened!" were not free enough, the gates were thrown open wide, and He stood there, the outstretched hand, instead of the door, the living friend, instead of the written words of welcome.

And as if that were not enough, instead of saying, "Come to me!" He came Himself—He "came to seek and to save that which was lost."

THOU AND I[3]

IN a room in a stately mansion, a little babe lay in its mother's arms. All kinds of beautiful things were around, and many people passed in and out. Pictures by the first Masters were on the walls; the rarest exotics filled the air with choice perfumes. The chair in which the mother sat was gilded and tapestried; the carpet her feet rested on was soft as mossy turf, and delicate as embroidery. Jewels sparkled on her dress.

The windows opened on a magnificent landscape, of park and lake, woodland and distant hills. But the little babe saw nothing but its mother's smile—understood nothing, but that it was on its mother's knee. Its only consciousness was "Thou and I!" and love.

*   *   *   *

The railway train was entering a long tunnel. The babe was still on its mother's knee. The darkness grew deeper. The heavy train thundered through the hollow earth. Another met it, and rushed past with a deafening din. An older child in the carriage screamed with terror. Many of the passengers felt uneasy, and were impatient to see the light again. But the baby cared nothing for the noise or the darkness. It looked in the dim lamp-light into its mother's face, and saw her smile, and smiled again. It knew nothing of the world but "Thou and I!" and love.

*   *   *   *

The ship was tossing fearfully on the stormy sea. Every timber strained, every wave seemed as if it must engulph the vessel. The weak and timid cried out in an agony of fear. The brave and loving moved about with white, compressed lips, and contracted brows, striving now and then to say some brief reassuring words to those for whose safety they feared. But the babe lay tranquil and happy in its mother's arms. Her breast was to it a shelter against the world. It knew nothing

---

[3] * Suggested by a passage in Sartorius' "Lehre von der heiligen Liebe," contrasting the world of a cold philosophy, "Ich and Nicht Ich," with the Christian's world, "Ich und Du."

of danger or fear. Its world was "Thou and I!" and love.

* * * *

Years passed away, and the baby grew into a child, and the child into a man. His life was one of many vicissitudes, of passionate hopes, and bitter sorrows, and wild ambition. He worshipped the world in many forms, and wandered farther and farther from the Father's house, until the world which first had beguiled him with its choicest things, came to feed him on its husks.

And a long way off, he thought of the Father and the home, and rose to return. His steps were doubtful and slow, but the heart which met him had no hesitation and no upbraidings. Then the wanderer understood the love with which he had been watched and pitied all those desolate years, the love with which he was welcomed now.

The earth, and sky, and human life grew sacred and beautiful to him as they had never been, because through them all, a living Presence was around him, a living heart met him; and, as of old on the mother's knee, once more, as he looked up to God his Father, his world became only "Thou and I!" and love.

His life moved rapidly on to its dark goal. He had to leave the sunshine of earth, its pleasant fields, and cherished homes, and all familiar things, forever. The light grew dimmer, and the darkness deepened. But he had no fear.

In the darkness, and the bewildering rush of new experience, he was again as the babe on the mother's knee. To him there was no darkness, no confusion. He looked into his Father's face, and smiled. Life and death and earth, all he left, and all he went to, were as nothing to him then. He had nothing but that one living, loving Presence, but it was enough.

Again it was "Thou and I!" and love.

And death found that childlike and angelic smile upon his lips, and left it there.

* * * *

A day will come of storm, and fire, and tempest, and convulsion, when earth and heaven shall mingle and be rolled up as a scroll and pass away. But in that day, what will such have to fear? Amidst all the convulsed worlds, the redeemed will rest tranquil as the infant in the storm on its mother's breast. For amidst it all, their eyes will rest on the Face which was bowed in death to save them, and will know no fear. It will be, "Thou and I, and Thou art love!" forever.

THE END